The Secret of Blackjack Woods

by

Ashlen Brown

TELEMACHUS PRESS

This book is a work of fiction. Names, characters, places and incidents are either the product of the author's imagination or are used fictitiously. Any resemblance to actual persons, living or dead, or to actual events or locales is entirely coincidental.

THE SECRET OF BLACKJACK WOODS

The publisher does not have any control over and does not assume any responsibility for author or third-party websites or their content.

Cover designed by Telemachus Press, LLC

Cover art:
Copyright © iStockphoto 12038061

Published by Telemachus Press, LLC
http://www.telemachuspress.com

ISBN: 978-1-939927-01-9 (eBook)
ISBN: 978-1-939927-02-6 (Paperback)

Version 2013.06.10

Printed in the United States of America

10 9 8 7 6 5 4 3 2 1

To my family.

CONTENTS

The Secret of Blackjack Woods

CHAPTER ONE
The Sighting

JIM THOMAS WAS sitting on the couch, watching TV in his family's living room. It was late in the summer evening, so there was no school to worry about for the twelve-year-old, and he was taking full advantage. He was laid out on the sleep-inducing couch and watching a repeat of one of his favorite cartoons, which he figured he was too old for, but he told himself he just liked to laugh at them. His dad, Jack, was already asleep so that he could get up early for work. Jim was glad he didn't have to go to sleep or wake up early these days because summer in Texas was amazing. These were the best days of the year.

A sudden crashing sound made him bolt upright, and he looked over to see the panicked faces of his mother, Karen, and eight-year-old sister, Jilly, as they flew through the front door. The family's dog, Banjo, was right with them, looking excited. He was a big Catahoula, gray with big, black splotches all over and white on his feet, chest, and the tip of his tail. He always looked like he was smiling and loved to chase rabbits if he could.

"What happened? Are you okay?" Jim asked.

He knew his little sister had a flair for dramatic shows, but to see his mom with a look of panic on her face was unnerving.

"We saw something out there!" Jilly answered.

Jim's little sister's eyes were as big as the moon, and she was breathing hard. Her little hands were trembling. She was looking back and forth between her brother and mom and shifting her weight as if to soothe herself.

Something had really shaken her up.

In contrast, his mother was extremely quiet. She was breathing a bit harder too, but she seemed extremely perplexed and a little worried. Banjo was sniffing his bed and getting ready to lie down now that the mysterious excitement was over.

"There was some sort of big animal out by the Jeep," Karen said.

Jim just stared. There were always animals, big and small, running around in the woods outside of their house. What made this different than those other times?

"What sort of animal? Was it a deer?" he asked.

Oftentimes, there were deer outside that let out extremely loud snorts and stomped their feet when alarmed. They would then go crashing through the woods. Even small animals like armadillos and raccoons could make huge crashing noises when they ran through the tall grass and bushes. Usually, that's what it was—a small animal making big noise.

"No. Definitely not," his little sister said. She seemed sure of it.

Karen and Jilly shared a look.

"Well, did you see it?" Jim couldn't figure out why it was so hard for them to say what it was.

"I did!" Jilly was still breathing hard and looked about to pop. "I saw something *huge* and something *hairy*. I think it was a were-wolf! It had shaggy hair and it walked upright, but bent over like this." She began to do a hunched sort of walk that reminded Jim of when he had sneaked and watched a werewolf movie that had secretly scared the daylights out of him.

"He was—"

"Wait a sec. '*He*'? How do you know it was a he?" Jim was smiling now.

"I don't! I'm guessing! He looked like a he, ya know?" She was looking exasperated with him. Like *come on*, of course it was a he! "I don't think he had a tail and he was sitting in the bushes by the Y in the driveway next to the Jeep. Waiting, I guess."

Their driveway split into a Y-shape with the left arm leading to the house and the right arm bending farther right and leading to their two-story garage. Their Jeep was currently sitting near the bend on the right arm of the Y just beyond where the two arms met.

Jim looked at Karen to confirm all of this and she nodded, she actually nodded! She was actually confirming this crazy talk!

"So we were walking to the Jeep, and he's waiting, and then we hear this *gurgling* sound. Like, like a stomach growling! And Mom goes, 'Jilly, is that you?' Like I could make that kind of noise! And I go, 'No, that wasn't me!' And right then I see him running across the driveway from the middle of the Y to that bend by the Jeep that has all that tall grass, and I screamed and then Mom and I ran and jumped into the Jeep! We left Banjo outside, of course."

She was huffing from the exertion of telling the story.

Karen piped up now.

"We waited in there, trying to figure out what it was until we figured it was safe. Then we got out and couldn't see anything, so we called Banjo and started to run back to the house. When we got to the Y in the drive, Banjo sniffed and his head jerked up and then he ran straight at the bend on the other side of us, and we heard this giant thing rush through the grass away from us!"

Jim was excited about this whole ordeal, although he didn't believe that it was anything more than a deer or something *explainable*. He thought it was still fun to kind of imagine and get excited about it, though.

"Then we called Banjo, and he actually followed us back to the house. It was like he knew it was something he shouldn't chase." Karen had finished and Jim saw she was waiting to see what he thought.

"It must have been a yeti!" His sister squealed as she said this and her hands flew up to her cheeks.

Jim was laughing now. "Maybe it was a ... WEREWOLF! OW, OWWWWW!"

His howling was quite convincing, and his sister shrank back from him with watery eyes. He was laughing really hard now.

Jilly did not think this was funny.

"Jim, you butt-head! I saw it and it wasn't anything I've seen before! I've lived here my whole life and never seen anything like that. Don't make fun." She blinked her eyes solemnly.

Jim wanted to see this thing. He jumped up from the couch and went for the door. "I'm going to see if it's still there."

"No, Jim! It'll eat you!" Jilly looked like she couldn't believe her brother was going out there. "Please don't!"

She was looking to their mom for help. Karen was looking at both of her kids and seemed to make a decision.

"Let's go." Karen had an adventurous streak, just like her son. Her eyes had the same gleam that Jim's held right now.

"Mom! What if he's still out there?" Jilly asked. Jim knew she couldn't believe her crazy brother and mother. "I'm going with you. I don't want to be in here alone if he comes back while you're out there."

"Dad's here," Jim pointed out.

"Dad doesn't wake up unless something really loud happens."

"This would be loud, I guarantee it." He sniggered.

"Jim!"

While they were bickering, Karen had found the big spotlight that they used sometimes to look at deer or other interesting critters when they wandered into their yard at night. The Thomas family loved the great outdoors and everything in it.

She gave Jim the light so that he could lead the way. They left Banjo inside since he was now fast asleep on his bed, snoring so loudly that Jim thought he probably wouldn't notice a snarling werewolf a foot away from him. Except that he always knew when raccoons were outside, even if they didn't make a sound. He would be sound asleep and just pop up with a snuffing sound, his face in the window. Jim loved that about him.

Armed with a light, the small group stepped outside onto the front deck of the house and walked up to the gate that led to the driveway. Jim wanted to be able to catch whatever this animal was if it had wandered back, so he opened the gate without turning on the light.

Standing for a few seconds to let his eyes adjust to the lack of light, he scanned the area. The moonlight from the nearly full moon was bright enough to give a blue glow to the parts of the driveway and woods not covered by trees. He could see from the left arm of the Y in the driveway to where the arms met and disappeared together in a wooded bend of the path. Looking to the left, he saw the smattering of bushes and trees that stood between the house and garage. They were small and not too thick to really hide much.

To the right was pure, heavy woods. Oftentimes, during the day Jim saw deer, rabbits, and squirrels. He had even seen coyotes skulking through there on their way to the thick part of their land, where he imagined they had a den. This was where he could picture a werewolf or bigfoot or *something* hiding out, but that's not where it had been.

Tonight, though, he could even see in these woods and nothing was there. Nothing that he could see, anyway, so he felt safe enough to venture out.

"Let's go, but be quiet." He looked at Jilly as he said this.

She was right behind him, and he knew it was because she wanted to be sandwiched between her big brother and her mom. Jim led them down the driveway to where they had seen this mystery creature.

He stopped and Jilly bumped into his back. "Shhh!" he hissed. His sister and mother seemed to be holding their breath. At least they were being quiet. He couldn't hear anything unusual, so he turned on the light. Shining it quickly, but methodically, he probed the two spots where he was told the animal had been seen. Nothing.

"So where was it? Go through it again," he said.

Jilly and Karen told the story again, but this time were able to walk through it as they told it. Jilly did an even better impression of the way it had walked, and Jim was starting to get more excited about the possibilities.

Of course, he didn't really think it was a werewolf or bigfoot like his sister did—she was positive about this—but he was starting to think that maybe it was a small black bear. He had heard on the news a few weeks back that black bears were making their way back into this part of the state. The prospect of seeing a real black bear was thrilling to Jim. He and his dad were hunters, so big game was exciting, but he also just loved wildlife and seeing a bear would be awesome.

He was hesitant to voice his idea of it being a bear in front of Jilly, but excitement got the better of him. "Maybe … it was a bear. What do you think?"

Jilly's face froze in a look of pure terror. She made a small squeaking sound. "That would be terrible! Hey! No way was that a bear! He was walking on two feet!"

"But bears sometimes rear up on their hind feet," Jim pointed out.

Karen had seen the same news stories, so she seemed to be mulling it over.

"Let's get inside," she said. "We'll talk to your dad about it tomorrow, see what he has to say. Enough excitement for the night."

And Jim *was* excited.

CHAPTER TWO
Strange Occurrences

THE NEXT DAY, Jim woke mid-morning. His dad was already at work, so he couldn't ask him about what had happened just yet. After a quick breakfast of cereal, Jim ran upstairs to his room.

Jilly was still asleep, so he couldn't ask her about her scary encounter the night before. He wanted to get a good description of what she had seen so that he could compare it to animals in the area. Sitting in his sleep shorts and t-shirt, his brown hair tousled, he figured he would get started without her and maybe have some pictures to show her later. He decided to look up bears on the Internet and see where exactly they had been spotted recently.

Doing a quick search, he found the news article about bears making their way back into the state of Texas, but they were mostly in West Texas, and Jim lived in the Southeastern part of the state. Maybe one had ventured farther east than usual, he thought.

There were also instances of people keeping big game animals hidden away on their property. He had heard about a tiger getting loose a few counties away sometime a while back. Maybe that's what's happening here.

Jim started mumbling through the physical description. "Five to six feet in length ... two to three feet high ... two to three hundred pounds ... color ranges ... longer front claws ... long and coarse fur."

He read that they generally avoid humans, but they can be very dangerous if provoked or feel threatened. He figured that was why it ran away—to avoid humans. Jim saved a picture of a black bear to show Jilly later and took some notes.

Reading on, he found out ways to tell where bears had been. This could be fun!

He decided that later he would go out for a hike and see if he could find any broken branches, stripped bark, or torn up ground. He knew that deer and other wildlife could make the same types of signs, but he would look anyway. This would be a challenge and he liked challenges. He also printed a picture of bear scat. He had just learned that "scat" was a term used for droppings and that people could tell what type of animal the scat came from. He might be able to try this out!

"What's going on, Jim? Any fun plans for today?" Karen was in the doorway with a basket of laundry to put away. She always liked to hear about his adventures and was known to help plan some.

"I'm looking up bears. This could be what you guys saw and heard. See?" He pulled up the picture of a black bear. This particular picture showed a young black bear reaching up on a tree to eat something, so it was on its back feet and sort of hunched like Jilly had described.

"Yeah, that could be it ... We'll have to show your sister, see what she says." She looked at Jim and then at the notes he had been taking and smiled. "My little biologist." She kissed his head, put his laundry on the bed and left.

Jim started looking through message boards of a website to
see if anyone had possibly seen the same thing close by. One post
caught his eye:

> I swear I saw a bigfoot! It was some big, hairy
> thing that walked right up to my back porch! My
> lights were off, so I didn't get a good look, but it
> was something right out of a movie!

Jim was excited. Maybe this was the same animal! He tried to
see where the person who posted the comment lived. All it said
was that he was from Central Texas, but that wasn't good enough.
Reading some responses, a couple of people seemed to humor the
blogger, but many were just plain rude. Jim thought about replying,
but he didn't want to seem crazy too, so he decided against it. He
would just do some research on his own and see what happened
for now.

He heard Jilly moving around in her room and went to see
what she thought of the matter. Walking down the hall toward her
room, he heard her stumble through the clutter she kept on her
floor and then she tumbled out of her door. Her eyes were
scrunched, and she seemed to still be half asleep.

"Hey," Jim said. She just looked at him for a moment and finally mumbled a soft "hey" back. She was not a morning person,
but Jim wanted to talk to her. "Come see what I've been working
on!" Jilly just stared, then rubbed her eyes and followed her big
brother to his room.

"This is an American black bear. Does it look like what you
saw?"

She rubbed her eyes again, harder this time, then opened them
really wide. "Uh, uh. That's not it."

Jim looked at her and felt sort of disappointed that he hadn't
solved the mystery. "Are you sure? Look again. See, they can be

five to six feet tall when they stand on their hind feet, they have long, shaggy hair, they're big, and look how this one's kind of hunched."

She looked again more alertly, but she still was adamant that this was not what she had seen. "Werewolf," was all she would say. She had obviously taken Jim's joke about it being a werewolf a little too seriously. Jim couldn't help but feel that this was his little sister being, well, a little sister. She must have exaggerated it in her mind. He really wanted this to be a bear.

Walking down the stairs, Jim felt slightly deflated, but still assumed Jilly was stretching things. He found Karen sitting at the kitchen table, doing some paperwork. Moms always have paperwork to do. Lucky for him, his school work didn't start back up for weeks.

"Mom, I'm heading outside." Jim always spent a lot of time outside in the summer. Most of the time, he took his sister along, but she was still waking up, and he was anxious to get outside today.

"Hey, honey?" Karen had put down her bills.

"Yeah, Mom?"

"Stay close."

"But, Mom! I haven't had to stay close for a while now. I'm not little anymore, and I know my way around the woods."

"Yes, but we saw something last night, and I want you close." She had a look in her eye that let him know she meant it.

Stepping out onto the back deck, Jim felt alive. He loved being outside. The smells, the sounds, the sights—everything. The Thomas family had a big, wooden back deck that reminded Jim of a boat deck. He liked to sit out there or walk along the railing and look out into their expansive backyard. Jim loved that he had twenty-one acres to explore. Fittingly, the Thomas family called their land "Blackjack."

Jack had cleared out a large area of their backyard, but there were still many trees and bushes, making it lush and private and distinctly wild. Looking straight back, Jim could just see part of the lake that wound down along their property line, delineating their property and a few of their neighbors' properties. The long and narrow lake ran perpendicular to their backyard, snaking left and right down their property line. It ended in a little creek to the right in front of their neighbor's home, so their part of the lake was very private, and they seemed to have it all to themselves.

Most of their land was to the left of the cleared portion of yard and had not been cleared out. It was untouched woods except for a few trails Jack had forged with his tractor. Over time, the paths had grown smaller, but they were well-worn by the family, especially Jim.

Jim wished he could explore this heavily wooded area and search for signs of a bear or something, but he walked down the steps of his deck and began his search closer to home. He walked along the tree line to the right first. This half-acre separated the Thomas home from their next-door neighbors, the Mayhews. In certain places, if the season was right and the trees especially sparse, Jim could see bits of his neighbor's house.

Walking this line, Jim looked around for any disturbed parts of the wilderness. He let his mind wander and found himself thinking about what it would be like to see a living bear. The only bear he had seen was a giant stuffed brown bear in a restaurant that was made to look like the old frontier at Disney World. He remembered sitting beneath that thing and thinking what an amazing animal it was.

As he walked from his house down the right tree line toward the lake, the only thing Jim saw was a ribbon snake. It was a rather long and fat ribbon snake, which would normally interest Jim greatly, but he had other things on his mind.

When he reached the lake, he walked along it across his yard to the other tree line and began walking back up to the house. As he did so, he vaguely became aware of a whooping sound. It initially didn't register because down the lake a ways was a family of boys who liked to be outside as much as Jim did. They were always out shooting BB guns and messing around, so he thought the whooping was coming from them.

Another "WHOOP" and this time Jim paid more attention. He stopped with his head tilted to the left, listening harder. He thought that the last one had come from the direction of his thick woods.

After five minutes, he hadn't heard it again, so he continued walking.

He looked to the "wood pile," as they called it, to his left. When the house had been built, trees had been cleared and piled up in the middle of what was now their backyard. Over the years, it had slowly melted into the earth, but it still contained trees and now mounds that Jim and Jilly liked to climb. They had even hidden a time capsule a couple of years ago in the dirt, where a fallen tree trunk had split and made a little hiding place.

While thinking about this, Jim heard another "WHOOP." It had definitely come from his right and fairly deep in the woods, where Jim knew it was thickest. He had no idea what that sound was—he hadn't heard it before. Oddly enough, though it almost sounded human, he had the distinct impression that it was not human. Jim didn't know any animal that sounded like that. Frowning, he wished Jack was home so that he could ask him about it. He made a mental note to ask him later.

The rest of his walk was uneventful, so Jim went inside to get Jilly. He thought she might be ready to go for a swim. When he opened the door, he heard his sister's voice talking to one of their cats. Her voice was high and squeaky, and she was talking to it like it was a baby.

Oh no, he thought.

Sure enough, when Jim entered the living room, he found Jilly sitting and their cat Jimmy dressed in a full suit and tie. Of course, she had pulled it off a stuffed teddy bear because, thankfully, she hadn't found a place that sold cat clothes. She had named him Jimmy after her big brother.

Poor Jimmy was sitting dutifully, but not looking too happy. She had him placed around a small tea set with some stuffed animals and was working on slipping a dress on their other cat, Oreo, who was not taking the idea of getting dressed as well as Jimmy had.

Banjo was lying next to the couch and watching the proceedings with what looked like a smile on his face.

"Aw, Jilly. Don't do that to them!" Jim hated it when she dressed them up.

"Why not, Jimsy?" She was smiling as she said this—partly because she was happy dressing up her cats, but partly because she liked teasing her brother about it.

"They hate it, and I hate it! Come on, take those things off them and let's swim."

"Yay, yay! I bet you a quarter I can beat you out there!" Jilly said.

Jim noticed a twinkle in her eyes.

"You're on!"

Jim and Jilly liked to race out to the pool, and Jim thought he could beat Jilly, but he hadn't counted on her already having her bathing suit on underneath her clothes. She had prepared. Jim caught sight of her running out the back door and realized his mistake.

He turned to head up the stairs and ran straight into his mother.

"Going for a swim?" she asked.

"Yep. Jilly won a quarter. I'm going to change."

"Okay, I'll go watch Jilly. Hurry up! And let Banjo into the side yard!"

By the time Jim got out to the pool, Jilly was already practicing her dives. She had some pool toys scattered in the pool, ready for them to play with.

Karen had gone down to the pool with her and was sitting on the bench of the deck, soaking up some sun.

"I think I'll join you guys," she said. "Jim, watch your sister while I change."

"Okay."

They began playing catch with their squishy water balls, and Jim told Jilly about the sound he had heard.

"Have you ever heard anything like that?" he asked.

The pool was seated along the right tree line about two-thirds between the house and the lake, and Jim looked across their back-yard to the tree line where he had heard the strange sound.

Jilly looked thoughtful for a moment and said, "No, I haven't. What do you think it was, Jimmy?" She liked to call him variations of his name—Jimmy and Jimsy were her favorites.

"I don't know, but I'm going to ask Dad."

After a few minutes, they heard the whoosh of the sliding glass door and saw Karen sit outside on the deck to talk to someone on the phone. It seemed like she was always getting stuck on the phone. She looked longingly out at them in the pool, but just smiled, waved, and went back to her conversation.

Jim began putting Jilly through drills with the ball. He was on the small seat in the deep end, and she was standing in the shallow end. He would throw bombs to one side or the other and make Jilly run and dive for them. She loved it.

Suddenly, they both heard a crashing sound coming from the heavy woods across the yard. They looked up and saw a small herd of deer bounding through their yard toward them. They veered off toward the lake and made their way past the pool, disappearing into the woods between them and the Mayhews. Banjo was barking excitedly from his spot in the fenced-in area on the side of their house.

Jim and Jilly looked at each other and then looked back up to the house, where Karen was standing and holding the phone down by her side.

"Did you see that, you guys?" She was excited. No matter how many times they saw a deer, they never tired of seeing them. They always loved it.

Jim, however, had a strange feeling. The way the deer were coming at them so recklessly, it seemed that they were running away from something. Usually, when they saw deer cross the yard, they were walking and eating grass here and there. Sometimes, they moved quickly and, usually, they were followed by some neighborhood dogs. This time, however, there was nothing behind them.

Jilly looked at Jim again and just shrugged. Jim started to shrug it off as well, figuring that some other animal scared them off, but then he started to wonder just what animal had scared them.

By the time they were done playing in the pool, they were wrinkled and tired. Karen had joined them just after the deer had disappeared, and she had given Jim a turn at trying to catch the balls. He was very good at anything related to sports and had enjoyed his time in the pool.

Later that evening, Jack had come home from work, and Karen and Jilly had told him the story of their encounter the night before. He had listened intently with a twinkle in his eye. Jack was tall and athletic with brown hair and kind, light brown eyes. In fact, people often told Jim that he looked just like his dad except for the eyes. Jim had steel gray eyes that often danced with his excitement. Like Jim, Jack enjoyed a good adventure.

"So what do you think it was?" Jack asked them.

"I think it was a werewolf," Jilly said very seriously.

Jack gave a small laugh, but not wanting to hurt her feelings, he asked, "Really? Who do you think it was? You know, the person it is when it's not a werewolf."

This hadn't occurred to Jilly because she scrunched up her face, thinking hard. "I don't know, but I would think that it would have to be somebody sort of close by because if he was caught out when he turned back into a man, he wouldn't want to be caught naked!"

The whole family couldn't help but laugh at this, even Jilly.

"So you think it's a man?" Jack asked.

"Yes."

"Yeah, Dad. Jilly says she just knew when she looked at it that it was a 'he'." Jim gave Jack a look that said everything. Like you could really know if a werewolf was a boy or girl just by looking at it, he thought. It's not like the girl werewolves would wear makeup and strings of pearls.

Jim gave Jack his idea about it being a bear. Jack scratched his chin in thought.

"I suppose that could be it. In all likelihood, it's probably just a dog or something like that. Sorry, Jilly."

He smiled at his little girl, who looked positively hurt by him not believing her, but she just said, "Hmph," and skipped off to find her cats, not seeming any worse for the wear.

Jim spent the rest of the night searching the Internet for sounds of the forest and to try to find out if a bear could make the sound he had heard. So far, no luck. Rubbing his burning eyes, he decided to go to sleep and get up early in the morning. He wanted to do some more research and hopefully go out and have a look around.

CHAPTER THREE
Back to Normal

THE EARLY MORNING sun streamed through Jim's window waking him up nice and early. He got ready for the day and went downstairs to find Karen making breakfast.

"Hey there. Get some good sleep?" she asked.

"Yeah, Mom. You?"

"Sure did. How about some pancakes this morning? I thought it would be fun."

"Sounds great! Let's not wake Jilly until I've had some first." He gave Karen a sly grin, and she just shook her head and called for Jilly. As early as it was, Jack had already run off to work, so it was just the three of them.

Jack Thomas owned a medical company that provided services to hospitals and doctors. He himself was a perfusionist. This meant that he ran the heart-lung bypass machine during open-heart surgery. Jim liked telling people that his dad kept people alive when surgeons were working on their hearts. This job meant early mornings, but he had some flexibility since he owned the company. Jim and his sister liked it when he surprised them at home during the summer days.

"Mom, can I go for a hike today?"

Jim was hoping that his mom felt less apprehensive about his exploring today than she had the day before, but she pursed her lips and said, "How about if we all go?"

This wasn't really what Jim had in mind because he had some serious work to do, but he always had fun when the family went exploring and this seemed to be the only way he would get to go.

"Sure! That will be good. I hope Jilly hurries, then."

Karen laughed at this because Jilly never hurried. Just then, Jilly hopped down the stairs, looking bleary-eyed, but grinning extremely excitedly.

"I LOVE pancakes! I get the first batch!"

"Uh, uh. Jim was up first. He already kind of asked if he could have the first ones." Karen nodded at Jim with a wink.

After a nice breakfast, they got ready for their excursion. Before they left, they all changed into their rubber boots to protect them from mud and, hopefully, snakes. Jilly had some pink rubber boots that Jim didn't think offered enough protection from snakes, but Jilly had insisted on getting them because they were "too cute!"

Again, Jim took the lead. He walked out the sliding glass back door and turned left on their expansive back deck. They all hopped off the edge of the deck and walked down the soft hill that their house rested upon. They left Banjo behind today, so that they could be quiet and maybe see some animals.

Jim was guiding them down their "water well trail" as they called it because it took them directly past their well and into the forest beyond. In this case, "beyond" was where Jim had heard the strange whooping noise the day before.

As they marched through the woods, all knew to be as quiet as possible. They had been through here many times in their lives and had always avoided noise so as not to scare away any wildlife. It was somewhat difficult in their clunky boots, but they were fairly good at it.

Nobody spoke.

This silence came from a desire to be quiet and from the beauty of where they were. Once inside the woods, Jim had always noticed that being quiet came naturally. He was always in such awe of the natural setting and always so alert for any interesting sights that he didn't seem to find much time for talk. However, there were those times when they broke into spirited talk and time seemed to stand still while they had amazing conversations about every topic imaginable.

As the leader, it was Jim's job to find the best path and to hold small branches aside for his sister, who was following closely behind him. He also had the big task of looking out for snakes. Since it was summer, snakes weren't uncommon.

After several minutes of walking, they came to a wider path that had been mowed out by their father. Over time, it had shrunk as the greenery had grown up a bit, but with regular use by both animals and the family, it was still an impressive path. If they followed this, it would wind through most of their property and take them to the backyard near the lake without too many scratches from branches and thorns.

They turned right on this path and traveled parallel to the house and backyard, heading toward the lake. The trail would soon wind left and back right. Despite the vast amount of ground they could cover on this trail, there were still areas of their acreage that were mostly untouched and hidden away. These were the areas that really interested Jim. He often found himself wondering what was hiding out in these places.

"Where are we going?" Jilly asked Jim.

"Just around. Seeing what's here."

He hadn't yet told his parents about what he had heard, but he still wasn't sure what it was anyway, so he didn't want to mention it now. It could have just been some nearby people and he would just be making a fuss out of nothing.

"I love the smells out here." Karen was looking around and breathing deeply. She saw Jim looking at her and smiled brightly. Jim liked how his mom always came alive being out here.

Karen was pretty and thin with long dark hair and tanned skin. Her eyes were dark brown and were shining now.

Just then, there was a loud crashing sound to their right. Jim's heart seemed to jump into his throat, and he felt tingly all over. Looking quickly to the right, Jim saw three deer, a mom and two fawns, bound through the bushes and deep into the woods away from them.

"Did you see that?" Jilly squealed excitedly. It was always a treat to see fawns. "Twins! That's so cool!"

"Isn't it? That was too special," Karen said in awe.

Jim was still standing there, staring in amazement at the spot where the deer had disappeared when he heard a growl behind him. It was a deep, guttural growl that was somewhere deep in the woods behind them. It sounded like an angry, sad, snarly growl. That direction would put it in one of those secret hidden places that they rarely explored. It sounded so far away that he almost didn't hear it, yet he was sure that he had. All of the hair on the back of his neck stood up.

"You hear that?" He looked at his mom and sister, who had been quietly chattering about the deer they had just seen and didn't seem to have heard anything unusual.

"Hear what?" Karen walked to where the deer had been lying and knelt down. "Look at where they were bedded down! The grass is all flat and still warm. Come see!"

"I heard a growl or something. Over there." Jim was pointing now and straining to hear it again.

"*I* didn't hear anything," Jilly proclaimed as she was squatted down, examining the deer beds. "Ohhh, little baby deer are so cute! See where they were sleeping? I couldn't even fit there, they're so tiny!" Squatted down like that, Jim thought she looked like just a pair of boots with a huge sheet of red hair attached.

Jim felt like maybe he was being paranoid. After all, since they had seen the strange creature, he had only heard a couple of noises that may or may not have been something unusual. He had no real reason to think that anything strange was going on or living in the woods, but he still couldn't shake the feeling that something was definitely up.

They continued on their hike with small smatterings of excited conversation about things they saw; interesting things like a beautiful butterfly, a giant grasshopper, and the tail-end of what looked like a big, black snake. Without a better look, nobody could say what kind it was, but it was big and looked dangerous enough.

Even with the excitement of the hike, Jim was slightly disappointed. He had heard a growl, but nothing more and nothing had been seen.

As the hike wore on, Jim started to think that the growl had probably been a large pig. Wild pigs had always lived in the area, particularly in their woods, and lately, they had seen an upsurge of activity.

Recently, they had even heard a large group of them just out of reach of the light from their front porch. They had heard loud grunts and snorts, and even some small squeals from young pigs. They had been close enough that they had even been able to smell a foul odor emanating from the dirty pigs. It made the most sense that the growl had come from a pig.

This thought greatly disappointed Jim.

By the time the group made it back to the house, Jim was almost feeling better about having been able to explain the sounds. This would mean he had been right last night. He even thought that perhaps the thing Karen and Jilly had seen was actually a pig. What if Jilly had just sort of exaggerated things in her head and it had been a pig making those gurgling sounds?

Jim started feeling pretty proud of himself. He also felt a bit silly, having made such a big deal about things, but that was fine. Jim was going to allow himself some sense of adventure and imagination this summer.

CHAPTER FOUR
Evidence Found

THE NEXT COUPLE of days were spent lazily enjoying summer with swimming, fishing, late nights of TV, and other such fun. Jim had spent the time not giving much thought to what had transpired previously, until one day he heard the neighbor boys across the lake talking loudly and excitedly. They were trespassing on private property, as they didn't own the property directly across from Jim's family, but that sort of thing happened a lot around here with no real problems. As long as nobody was hunting or doing anything dangerous or illegal, most people with large amounts of land didn't mind too much.

Jim had been lying on the hill of dirt that separated the pool from the lake area, playing with a magnifying glass. He had been looking at a particularly strange-looking beetle that had what looked like two small horns above its eyes. This gave it a rather dinosaur-like appearance, and Jim was studying it with curiosity.

"What do you think made those marks?" Jim's youngest neighbor was asking. His name was John Whittle, and he was a year younger than Jim and several inches shorter with dirty blonde hair and blue eyes.

His older brothers, Sam and Dave, were two and three years older than Jim, respectively. They were about the same size, which was a few inches taller than Jim, and of medium build. These two looked more like twins than not. They both had brown hair and liked to wear mean sneers on their faces most of the time. This was because they liked to play soldier and acted like they were tougher than anyone else and more skilled, but they were pretty dangerous.

Once, Jim had seen Dave accidentally shoot Sam in the butt with his pellet gun while they were pretending to save a "hostage," a neighbor girl, from a "terrorist," played by John. They seemed to like Jim, so he stayed on friendly terms with them, but did not seek out their company.

Sam answered, "Got no idea, but these look like they're from claws, see?"

Jim could hear them murmuring now and couldn't quite make out the words. He slowly lifted up on his hands slightly so that he could see over the hill and to where they were crouched. He could just make out the tops of their military-style buzz cuts crowded around something in the mud on the bank of the lake.

Jim wanted to know what they were looking at, but was hesitant to alert them to his presence. If only they would talk louder …

"See this, it's where it walked up and slid a little. You can see the claws there—they're massive!" Dave's voice had become louder with excitement and, again, was carrying to Jim's hiding place. "Where are its front feet? I guess it stepped where it wouldn't leave prints …" His voice trailed off with his uncertainty.

Now Jim was really curious. Despite telling himself that everything that had happened was just coincidence and very explainable, here were three other people who had found something unusual. He had to find out what it was.

"Hey, guys. What's up?" He had popped up and was walking down the hill toward the pier on his side. The three buzzed heads turned quickly to Jim.

"Hey there, Jim. Didn't see ya," Sam said. "We've found something here. A print of some sort. Looks like a big animal with claws. Might be some good huntin' tonight!" He had a gleam in his eye.

The Whittles loved hunting, but probably more to inflict pain on animals smaller than them rather than for the sport or to obtain food. They had a dark quality that rarely showed itself, but when it did, it disturbed Jim.

Once, Jim was sure that he had witnessed Dave trying to hit a raccoon with his ATV for fun. When Jim had confronted him, Dave had seemed perturbed and claimed the swerve had been an accident.

"See anything else?" Jim asked.

"Hair here! Looks kinda long … What's it from, Sam?"

John had found some hair clinging to the barbed wire fence that stood a few feet back from the edge of the lake. There was a small stretch of fence that separated out part of their neighbor's land to keep his large, white dog safely confined. The rest of his land was unfenced.

"I dunno. Maybe deer? From like a winter coat?" Sam was guessing.

"Maybe, but nah … looks too long and shaggy." Dave was examining it now. "Maybe," he concluded.

"Let me come see," Jim shouted over. He was now very curious about their findings. He hopped into his family's jon boat and began paddling across the lake, which was only about eighty feet across. As he pulled up to the bank, Sam grabbed the rope in the front of the boat and helped pull him ashore several feet to the left of the prints they were examining.

"Thanks," Jim said, hopping out.

Standing on the other side of the lake, the first thing that struck Jim was a pungent smell. It was one of those smells that is obviously only just lingering, but had been strong at one time. It reminded him of the wild pigs he had smelled, but not quite. Still, it was musky and ... *feral*.

He walked over and bent to take a look at the tracks first. In the mud by the water, there appeared to be two footprints that seemed to step away from the water and into the grass at the edge of the lake.

"They look kinda like a big cat paw print, see? But they kinda look funny. Maybe he slid in the mud a bit ... made them look longer," Sam guessed.

Jim peered closely at the tracks. What Sam said could make sense, but to him, they looked more like the ball of a human foot. But what person walked around here barefoot? Maybe the neighbor had to take his boot off for some reason and made a jump from his boat?

The prints were sort of rounded and there were obvious toes, but it was hard to tell exactly how many or if they were the smaller toe pads of a big cat because they had sunk into the mud. It almost looked like the middle part of the foot as well, but there was no heel mark, as if this person had pushed up on the ball of the foot to climb the slightly slanted bank of the lake. Near where toes might be, there were marks in the mud that looked like claws. Or maybe nails, Jim thought, but he didn't know anyone with such long nails.

Dave cut into Jim's thoughts. "Come look at this hair. What do you make of it?" He was standing next to the barbed wire fence that was a few feet back from the lake. There was a slight depression in the earth beneath the lowest wire that was obviously where small animals, and perhaps deer, slid under the fence to get to and from the lake. These animals had worn the grass away and created a trail through the grass on either side.

The fence had three strands of barbed wire with the top strand standing at about four feet high. The tuft of hair was

suspended on the top strand. Jim couldn't quite put a finger on
what it reminded him of. He knew it looked like something he had
seen before, but it wasn't coming to him at that moment. It was a
few inches long, coarse, and it was the reddish-brown color of a
deer in the deep summer months.

"Looks like deer hair," Jim said, "but longer."

"That's what I thought," Dave agreed.

"Could have come through running away from the cat!" John
said. He thought that the prints were from a large, predatory cat of
some sort.

"Hey, yeah. That makes sense," Dave said. "It's probably a
cougar. They're making a comeback around here, and they can take
down deer. It probably was hiding down here by the water and
chased the deer *under* the fence while it went *over.*"

His eyes were gleaming. Jim wasn't sure, but he thought that
Dave seemed to like the idea of a big cat chasing and killing a deer.

Jim was quiet. He definitely did not think the footprints belonged to a cat, and he was sure the hair was too long for a deer,
but he said nothing. His lack of agreement, however, seemed to
irritate Dave, who was looking at him with a smug expression on
his face that Jim always hated. This guy seemed to think he was
great and that everyone should agree with him.

"What? You don't think that's what it is?" Dave was starting
to look less smug and more upset. He was challenging Jim to
disagree.

"I'm just not sure that the prints look exactly like cat prints.
Maybe they are, though, who knows?"

He wanted to keep things casual and calm, and certainly not
tell them about the other odd things he had heard and what his
mom and sister had seen. To soften things, he added, "We can
look up different cat prints online and see. How about that?"

This seemed to mollify Dave, whose smug look had returned.

With tensions lessened, Jim took out the cell phone his parents had bought him and snapped a quick picture of both the prints and the hair. He took them from different angles and used his own foot to get a perspective of the size.

As he did so, he realized just how big the foot that made the prints had to be. Whatever it was, the animal was big.

"Look at the detective here," Sam said, but he said it more in an admiring way.

The brothers knew Jim was smart and this fact seemed to irk Dave, but the other two appreciated his intelligence. There had been times when his quick thinking had helped them out of a jam in the past. He had also been able to help them fix an old dirt bike they had with some tinkering and some Internet help.

Jim just laughed lightly and gave an appreciative nod. He couldn't help but notice that the prints looked as if something had come across the lake and walked out of the water, crossed the fence, snagging hair behind, and walked into the woods. If that was true, it, whatever *it* was, had come directly from his own woods.

Later that night, Jim lay in bed, thinking about what he had seen. He started with his sister's account of what she had seen a few nights ago, even though he wasn't entirely sure that her account was accurate. It was something she had never seen before and was not able to readily identify. It was fairly tall, walked upright with a hunch, had long hair, and made a "gurgling" noise. The next day, he had heard that weird whooping noise, and after that, he had heard a growling sound in the hidden areas of his woods. Now today, he could add a footprint and some strange hair.

Even though he was getting more and more curious about these events, Jim couldn't help but think that each of them could be completely unrelated and completely natural. That didn't keep

the nagging feeling that they were all connected and meant something very different and exciting from snaking its way into his mind
and taking hold.

He was going to figure this out.

CHAPTER FIVE
Turned Upside Down

BARKING WOKE JIM up early the next morning. He jumped out of bed and ran to look out his window and see what was making so much noise. Looking out over the backyard from his corner window, Jim could see the Mayhews' three big dogs running wildly across his yard toward their house. The large white one was running in circles around the black one and the brown one, all while barking his head off. He seemed to be herding them from Jim's deep woods on the left, across his yard, and back to their house at the right.

He watched them disappear into the wild, thick bushes and wondered what had excited them like that. Jim washed up for the morning, threw on his camo shirt and some olive cargo shorts, and ran downstairs.

Jack had already begun his long commute into town, and Karen and Jilly were already eating breakfast. Jim grabbed an apple and a granola bar and headed for the door, where he started putting on his boots.

"Mom, I'm going outside for a bit. Might go for a hike."

Sensing a slight hesitation, he looked at Karen, but she smiled and told him to have fun and be careful. "Stay within earshot," she warned.

That was something he could do.

Today, Jim was going to put in some time looking for the creature that had been sneaking around and causing trouble. He had come up with a great idea before he fell asleep last night. There was a tree just off the water well trail that would be a perfect spot to sit and watch the woods. He had packed a small bag with the binoculars that Jack had bought him for his last birthday, his snacks, some water, and a small digital camera. He was going to be prepared.

As he stepped up to the door, Banjo came bounding up to him, looking excited. Jim knew he wanted to go too. He was looking up at Jim with his huge eyes and wagging his tail so hard that his whole body shook. Jim felt bad about leaving him, but he wanted to be able to watch for his mystery animal. He bent down, patted Banjo on the head and said, "Sorry, boy. I'll be back, and I promise to take you for a nice walk later." Making sure that nobody was watching, he kissed him quickly on the top of the head and went out the door.

After a few of minutes of hiking, Jim came to the tree. It was situated off all the trails with a view of the water well trail and the other trail that intersected it and wound through the rest of the property. The tree had two boards nailed into the thick trunk that Jim could reach by raising up on tiptoe and pulling himself up with his arm strength. They had apparently been nailed on by the land's previous owner, who may have used it as a deer stand from which to hunt.

The best thing about this tree was that the trunk split off into two main parts. One veered slightly to one side, but mostly straight up, and split into many branches full of leaves. The other part swerved far to the side and was almost horizontal. This large branch was split open to make a sort of curved shelf that Jim could actually fit inside. It reminded him of a hammock.

Another fun feature was a smaller tree that was growing straight up beside the split base of the trunk and was the size of a fireman's pole. Jim had tried to slide down it like a pole once, but even though the trunk was fairly smooth, it had not been smooth enough to slide without gloves or at least using long sleeves to wrap his arms around the trunk. He had found that out the hard way.

Jim pulled himself up the steps and climbed over the split in the trunk to reach the open hammock branch. He had grown since the last time that he had rested in the branch, but he still fit nicely. After making sure there were no bugs hiding in there with him, Jim slid his legs into the partly closed base of the branch and settled into the spot, propping himself up on his left arm so that he could look over the lip of the shelf and watch for anything below. From this vantage point, Jim could see a good way off through the woods, and he could see parts of both of the trails.

Several minutes passed, and Jim had seen nothing interesting. He could hear birds chirping, hawks screeching from above, and little critters running around in the grass below. Once or twice he saw squirrels chasing each other high in the trees. They were screeching madly at each other and running along the branches, jumping wildly from one tree to the next. Jim admired the way they could balance and easily move along a thin branch and then hurtle themselves through the air, grab hold of another tiny branch, and continue like it was nothing.

It was coming up to an hour when he felt the phone in his pocket vibrate. Since the service near their house was spotty, his family used text messages to communicate and this one was from his mom. She was checking on him, so he assured her that he was all right. He told her he was seeing some cool stuff and had heard a hawk. Karen liked hawks and birds of all kinds.

As he was texting her, Jim became aware of a smell that he realized was growing stronger. It had been very faint at first, and he almost hadn't noticed it, but it was becoming very hard not to notice.

Jim was trying to figure out what the smell was when he felt a tickle on his right arm. He turned his arm over and saw a huge black spider crawling up it. Jim was a brave young guy and could handle most anything, but spiders were one thing he couldn't stand. He liked seeing them, but never wanted to touch one and this one was having fun putting its hairy legs all over his arm.

Jim froze for a second and then exploded with disgust, flinging his arm to try to dislodge the spider, but it fell on his side instead and started clambering up toward his neck. Without thinking, Jim started to jump up, but his legs were still lodged in the tree. He twisted to try to get the spider to fall off his shirt and over the lip of the branch, but his balance was off, and he felt himself falling over the edge of the shelf.

Completely forgetting about the spider, Jim flailed his arms wildly, looking for something to grab hold of, but because the branch was split, there was nothing to grab. He looked at the pole-like tree and tried frantically to grab it and right himself, but he was too far away, as it was situated near his feet, and he began to topple over the edge.

In a sickening moment of realization, Jim knew that he was going to fall headfirst out of his hiding place. In an instant, he fell. He had no time to yell out, as he fell too quickly. He saw the ground zoom toward him. In a fraction of a second, he felt a sharp yank on his right leg, and he stopped falling with a hard jerk.

In his efforts to stop himself from falling, he had kicked his left leg free, but his right leg had become wedged in the split hammock branch. He felt a hot pain in his ankle and knee. When he could begin thinking again, Jim realized that he was now dangling upside down from the branch with his back to the tree and his right knee bent at a ninety-degree angle.

Panic seized his chest, and his heart started thumping hard against his ribs. He felt like he couldn't breathe, and his vision started to get fuzzy. Finally, he remembered to try to yell for help, but his voice came out in a croak. He managed to get out a hoarse "help," but he was sure nobody could hear him.

It was then that Jim felt like he was slapped in the face by the most pungent smell he had ever encountered. It was the musky, feral scent he had smelled before, but multiplied by a hundred. He could smell dirt, musk, and sweat all mixed together. The smell sharpened his mind and brought him out of the panic that had almost frozen him.

He managed to yell for help in a stronger voice and began trying to look around for what was producing the smell. Yelling again, he twisted to his right to see if there might be a wild pig nosing around in the dirt nearby and felt the icy hand of panic grip him again. The "help" he had been about to yell froze on his lips, and he felt his heart hammer in his chest again. That tingly feeling of fear shot through his entire body. His eyes were popping out of his head at the sight before him.

Standing there, in the middle of a small clearing twenty feet away, was something he had never seen before. It was at least six feet tall and standing upright like a man, but it was covered in that same reddish-brown hair he had seen on the barbed wire fence—from head to giant foot.

It stared at him with large, brown eyes, and its nostrils were flaring as it moved its chin forward and sniffed his scent. Jim could hear its loud inhalation. It was a sound that made every hair on his body stand on end. Its feet were huge and covered with hair, and Jim could see thick, yellow nails that had grown over the ends of the toes into rounded points.

Only one word came to Jim's mind—bigfoot.

Twisted as he was, Jim was starting to cramp up, but he was too scared to unwind himself and take his eyes off this thing. His mind started working yet again, and he was able to start yelling for help, but it sounded feeble, even to Jim.

He tried to thrash himself free and reach up to grab his leg, all at the same time. The blood had been rushing to Jim's head and was threatening to make him black out. The bigfoot made things worse, and Jim was terrified that he would pass out and the thing would get him.

Just as this thought entered his head, the thing actually took a tentative step forward. Jim immediately stopped his frantic thrashing. They stared into each other's eyes for what seemed like forever to Jim and then it started walking slowly up to him as he dangled helplessly. Something instinctive told Jim to stay still. He watched it approach and noticed that the smell grew even more powerful, making his eyes water.

When it was five feet away, it stopped again and looked at Jim. Its eyes left Jim's face and traveled up to where his leg was trapped in the tree. The thing reached its arm up toward Jim.

Just then, he could hear Karen yell his name.

The thing whipped its head around and then looked back at Jim. What was strange was that Jim could then see some fear enter the creature's eyes. Jim still couldn't seem to yell. He heard Karen getting more frantic and then he heard her footsteps pound across the deck. He knew that she would be running along the trail now to find him.

This thought made him feel better and more scared all at once. He was desperate for Karen to help him, but he was afraid because she didn't know what was waiting here for her. What if it turned on her?

The bigfoot looked at Jim again, and he could see it come to some sort of decision. It started walking straight up to Jim and reached its arms up high. Jim let out a small yell and started to throw his arms out for protection, but the thing made an impatient grunt and ignored him as if nothing he could do could hurt it.

It reached past Jim's arms and grabbed his leg above his knee, then grabbed Jim's left arm at the bicep. Lifting Jim up as if he weighed very little, the thing dislodged his foot and set Jim down roughly on the ground. It let go of Jim and looked at him for a second longer, then turned, and with big strides, retreated quickly into the woods.

Jim heard a crashing sound and Karen's frantic yells. She broke through the bushes and turned her head, searching for a sign of her son. She ran down the trail, still looking for Jim. When she saw him, she let out another yell and ran to him with fear etched over her face.

"Jim! What happened?"

Jim still couldn't speak. He was in shock over what had just happened. He let out a little noise and then cleared his throat.

"Are you okay? Say something!" She began running her hands over his limbs and body, trying to find injuries. She was a retired nurse, so this was second nature to her. She quickly found his now swollen knee and ankle and began palpating for breaks.

"Mom! Mom. I saw … I'm okay." He couldn't yet put into words what had just happened. He didn't know how to tell her.

"What happened? Jilly heard you yell for help and ran in to tell me. I got here as fast as I could. Your knee is wrecked."

"I fell out of the tree, but caught my leg up there. I was hanging for a while. It's just my leg that's hurt."

Karen looked up at the spot that had trapped him and back down at him.

"Why didn't you answer me? I was scared to death." She was gripping him under the arms now to help him stand on his good foot. Jim winced at the pain.

"I … was scared and … I saw something."

Karen looked at him with concern. "What did you see?"

"I … I don't know. I was just hanging upside down too long. It was nothing. I don't even know what I'm saying. Let's just get back."

They walked in silence back to the house. It took a while with Jim's hurt leg, but by the time they reached the house, Jim could put a little bit of weight on his leg. He could tell it was sprained at the knee and ankle, but he thought it would be okay with time. It would be really sore tomorrow, but it would heal.

As they reached the back deck, Jilly launched herself at him.

"Oh, Jim! I was so scared! I heard you yelling, and you sounded so weird and scared, and I just couldn't take it! I thought you were dead!" Her big hazel eyes were full of tears. She was clutching his hand with her tiny hands.

Jim couldn't help but smile. She could be so dramatic, but when he thought about what had just happened, he thought she was right. He could have died—either from the fall or from the bigfoot. Of course, he wouldn't tell them that.

"Well, you have some bruises and cuts, and I'm sure you've sprained some things, but I'm really glad it wasn't worse," Karen said. She gave him a fierce look that told him she had pictured many worse scenarios and was not happy about being put through that. "I hope you didn't tear anything. Maybe we should go get you checked out." She helped him through the back door.

"No, Mom. I'm fine." He didn't want to go to the hospital or doctor's office and have to tell them this story. Limping along with Karen, he made it to the living room.

She cleaned up his cuts and got him set up on the couch with some ice. Jilly was perched on the edge of the couch, beside him. Banjo had been on top of him since he came back inside. He was staring at Jim with those soulful eyes and he just seemed to sense that everything was wrong. His nose started working furiously, and Jim knew he could smell the bigfoot on him.

"What happened, Jimmy?" Jilly was wringing her little hands again.

Jim didn't want to scare her, but Karen asked, "What did happen, Jim?" as she leaned on the back of the couch and looked down on him.

He took a deep breath and told them what had happened, but he made up a fantastic escape that involved a bit of acrobatics and using the pole tree to get himself down. He said nothing of the bigfoot.

Jilly made little gasps and squeals as he told his story. When he finished, she looked scared and Karen looked shocked.

"You idiot, Jim! You could have fallen and landed on your big, stupid head!" Jilly had a way with words, but Jim knew that she just expressing her love in her own way.

"Thank goodness you're okay," Karen said. She had a look on her face that told him she knew how lucky he was.

"Yeah, well I'll be sore later." He fell back onto the couch.

"I can't believe my big brother freaked out over a little spider." Jilly snorted at this.

When Jack came home, Jim had to tell his story again. For the second time, he didn't mention the thing that had saved him.

He hobbled upstairs after dinner and sat himself in front of his computer, careful to prop up his bad leg. It was really starting to hurt now. The throbbing seemed like it might become unbearable overnight.

Jim wanted to research bigfoot. He was absolutely sure that was it. A hairy man? That's bigfoot.

A cursory search brought him to some websites that had supposed pictures of the hairy beast. They were generally what he had seen, but none appeared to be authentic to Jim. His bigfoot was more … *real*. His bigfoot may have vaguely reminded him of an ape of some sort, but it also had a more human quality.

Jim kept repeating what had happened in his mind. He remembered peering into this creature's eyes and seeing some sort of understanding. The more he thought about it, he was sure that it had been motioning to him as it approached. He remembered it walking up to him with its arm reaching up high. It had looked like it was pointing before reaching up and grabbing him. The thing had actually tried to convey the message that it wanted to free him.

Amazing!

Looking at a recent article, Jim saw that some people believe that bigfoot may be an ape species dating back one hundred thousand years ago, but the thing in the picture was too ape-like. Whatever Jim had seen was more human.

Many people had uploaded sounds that they claimed came from bigfoot, and Jim now clicked on these links. The first sound he chose was a deep grunting noise. Jim thought it sounded like a pig, but who knows. The next sound made Jim's spine tingle. It was the whoop he had heard a few days ago—exactly what he had heard!

He went to another sound and it was shocking. Some people claimed that they heard strange gurgling sounds when they had seen a bigfoot. It was just as Jilly had described.

Jim spent another hour researching bigfoot, but there had been no reported sightings in his part of the state, that he could find. Most of what he found was conjecture. There was nothing really substantial. Jim couldn't help but wonder if any of these people had actually seen a bigfoot like he had. Were the stories real? Could he find someone who really had seen one and share his story?

For now, Jim thought it was best to keep all of this to himself. He wasn't sure what he would do with this information, but he knew one thing—he wanted to see bigfoot again.

CHAPTER SIX
Watching

THE NEXT MORNING, Jim woke slowly and late. He was groggy and more sore than he had ever been in his whole life. His knee was three times its normal size and throbbing. His ankle was no better, but it didn't feel as bad as his knee. The scrapes on his leg were threatening to split open with every movement. They had that tight feeling every time he moved.

Uncomfortable as he was, Jim showered and got ready for the day. He hobbled downstairs, relying heavily on the railing and clunking quite noisily. Karen had apparently heard his slow progress and met him at the base of the stairs.

"How's the leg?"

"Fantastic."

Karen was used to sarcastic answers from Jim and gave a knowing smile.

"That bad, huh?" She reached out to help him to the couch, and Jim didn't protest.

"Well, it's pretty sore, but it'll be okay soon enough."

Karen started fussing around him, getting his couch pillows all stacked and settled, and bringing the TV remote closer. "Want something to eat?"

"Sure. Anything sounds good."

"Anything it is."

As Karen left, Jim started to feel confined. He wanted to get outside more than anything right now, but his leg injury prevented it. He also knew that Karen wouldn't want him out there by himself for a while after what happened last time. Somehow, he would have to make her trust him again.

After a nice breakfast of eggs, sausage, and orange juice, Jim fell back on the couch, flipping through the TV channels. He came to a wildlife show and got comfortable.

A few minutes into a program about wolves and how they hunt their prey, Jim noticed that Banjo had popped up from his giant bed by the front window, crossed the room, and was looking out the side window that overlooked the water well trail.

Jim didn't think much of it at first. Banjo was always smelling and hearing things long before anyone ever actually saw them—if they ever got to see them at all. Usually, he only got really excited if he saw a raccoon or two climb the fence to eat cat food on the front deck. Banjo hated it when they did that. He would growl like some giant, menacing beast and try to paw at the window. His barks during a raccoon invasion would raise anyone's hair. Banjo could really be scary to someone who didn't know he was such a sweet dog—or if they were a raccoon.

This time was different, though. He was looking out the window quite intensely and sniffing so loudly it was making it hard for Jim to hear the TV.

With some effort, Jim got up and walked over to Banjo. He noticed Banjo's fur was raised, and he was baring his teeth with a low, deep growl.

"Hey, boy. What's out there?" he asked, stroking the dog's head.

Banjo jumped at his touch, apparently unaware of his approach. He was too focused on whatever he could see or hear. Or maybe smell. He looked up at Jim quickly and gave him a small lick.

"What's up with Banjo?" Karen had heard the low growl.

"I guess he sees a raccoon or something. He's a good guard dog, huh?"

"The best." She returned to the kitchen.

Jim had a feeling that it was more than just a raccoon out there. He was sure it was his bigfoot and that it was now coming closer to his home.

A voice made Jim jump.

"Jimmy! Let's do something." Jilly had come down from her room, where she had been playing with her Barbies for most of the day. Jim just couldn't understand how Barbies could keep someone interested for that long.

"Okay, but nothing where I have to move too much."

Looking at Banjo again, Jim saw that even Jilly's boisterous presence hadn't shaken his focus. He was sure he knew what was bothering Banjo. Gingerly bending down by his dog, he whispered, "I know, boy. I know it's out there. But I'm not sure it's so bad. Not yet anyway."

After a few days of rest, Karen suggested something that made Jim wince—wince worse than his leg. She suggested going over to the Whittle's house. She and their mom, Tess, were on friendly terms, much like the boys, but not really friends. Still, they spoke over the phone here and there. Apparently during the last conversation, Tess had suggested that all the boys get together.

While Jim sometimes liked hanging out with them and doing guy stuff, they were starting to really get on his nerves. In their younger years, they were fairly close friends. One summer, they were inseparable. But these guys were just, well, *weird* sometimes. And Dave was starting to act dumb around him and seemed to always be challenging him. The recent confrontation over the footprints was becoming more of their typical encounter.

"Mom, I think I should wait until my leg's completely better. They'll want to walk through the woods and stuff, and I can't."

Even though his leg was much better, he was trying anything to get out of this right now. He really wanted to do some more research on bigfoot and maybe sit outside and try to hear something.

"Come on. They're a decent family." She added, "Generally."

Karen seemed to share his feelings about the Whittles, but she still tried to have him visit them once in a while since he didn't have a brother. Jim thought that she also worried about his lack of friends sometimes.

While Jim was well-liked by almost anyone he met, he didn't have many close friends. He didn't mind. He liked messing around in the woods by himself and, lame as it may sound, he liked his family. His best friend was currently on vacation with his family. They would be gone the whole summer, so Jim was on his own.

Karen continued, "Mrs. Whittle said she was going to make pizza and they wanted to show you some new stuff they got. I think it's paintball gear."

"Okay, that sounds cool."

The paintball gear had perked Jim up. He was good at paintball. A natural, even. He had played at a course a few times with Jack, his uncle and cousin, and some family friends. Jim was an excellent shot and had good instincts. When it came to Capture the Flag, he was unstoppable.

The last time he had played paintball, though, he had gone with the Whittle brothers. They had played a few rounds and decided on the last game to split up and have two on each team, so they could play against each other. Jim had played with Sam, and Dave had played with John.

At first, they were all too busy contending with the other people playing to notice each other, but eventually it had come down to them and a few other people who were either lucky or as good as they were. They all were playing seriously, but still laughing whenever they spotted each other and one of them got a close shot. Finally, Jim had flanked Dave and John and had shot Dave right in the back.

Jim and Sam had busted out laughing, and when John saw what had happened, he had cracked up too. They had assumed Dave would laugh like usual, but he had been furious. Jim had never seen Dave like that before. He had turned bright red and started yelling about Jim cheating. For the rest of the day, Dave wouldn't look at Jim and made the rest of the group feel very uncomfortable.

Of course, Jim knew he was just mad that he had lost, but the fact that he got so angry when Jim beat him was not lost on Jim. He was getting very competitive with Jim for some reason, and Jim didn't like it. The next time he saw him, though, Dave had acted like nothing happened.

Despite their last paintball encounter, Jim liked paintball and paintball gear, so he was interested.

Karen drove Jim over to the Whittle house around lunchtime the following day. When they pulled into the long driveway, two big, slobbering mutts ran up to the car barking. Jim always found them annoying, but he never said anything.

Tess appeared in the front doorway and tried unsuccessfully to call off the dogs and then ushered Karen and Jim into the house.

"Hello! Hello! How's the leg, Jim? Your mom told me about your ordeal. How scary! I'm glad you're okay."

She said all of this while busily shuffling through the house and picking at little things here and there, as if anything was out of place and actually needed attention. Their house was sparse and clean, with none of that extra stuff that really seemed to make a house a home.

Tess was tall and of medium build. She had light brown hair, worn in a style that looked to Jim to be somehow a bit old-fashioned, although he couldn't put his finger on why that was. She also wore a lot of face makeup that made her look like she was constantly wind-burned. At least, that's what Jim thought. She was always nice to him, though.

"Thanks, Mrs. Whittle. Where are the guys?"

He didn't want to give her the opportunity to make him go into detail about what had happened to his leg, so he edged toward the back door since he assumed the guys would be in the backyard.

"They're out back, sweetie," she replied. Turning to Karen she said, "You just have to see what I bought the other day!"

Jim knew that Karen had wanted to quickly drop him off, but she was now trapped for at least an hour.

Slipping out the back door, Jim could see the guys down by the lake across their long stretch of backyard. They had made a shooting range down there for practicing with their pistols and they had also made a crude paintball course. It consisted of scraps of wood made into little huts and shielding walls, and piles of wood trimmings and tree logs left over from yard work. It was pretty great to Jim.

Limping a bit, Jim crossed the distance fairly quickly and could now hear Dave. "It's just like the ones they use in the Army. I can fire about twenty balls per second."

Jim knew this was fast for a semi-auto paintball gun, so Dave probably couldn't shoot that fast.

"Well, the ones in the Army shoot bullets, Dave." Sam was grinning.

"I know that," Dave snapped.

Jim couldn't afford an expensive paintball gun or anything extra, but he didn't need anything more than his inexpensive gun to beat most people. Once a shooter gets a gun that isn't the single pump type of gun little kids start off with, it really just comes down to skill. Either they have it, or they don't. And Jim had it.

"Hey, Jim! How's it going?" John looked excited to see him, and his eyes immediately went to Jim's leg.

Jim braced for their questions.

"Heard about your tree accident." Dave was smirking. "Those trees can really kick your ass if you aren't careful."

"Yeah, well you should see the tree. He's in far worse shape," Jim quipped back. He was trying to keep things light.

Sam roared with laughter, and John couldn't help but join in. Jim got the feeling that they liked it when someone else got the better of Dave these days.

"Let's see the new gun, Dave. Looks nice."

This seemed to mollify Dave for the time being, who began barking out orders for the day's activities. Apparently, they had planned for the four of them to go through drills to practice different battle situations.

"You never know when we'll be under attack and will have to know this stuff," Dave said. "When we are attacked, the four of us will be able to defend our families."

Sam and John nodded, but Jim was wondering just who was going to attack and why.

They had elaborate plans and were extremely serious about their "training." The three boys turned hard-faced and were quick to yell when Jim didn't perform properly, which was often with his bad leg and because he didn't have his heart into it today.

Jim's patience was waning after an hour of Dave's moody behavior. The brothers were now having a shooting contest with their paintball guns. He sat on a tree stump next to the water and watched the lake. He liked to watch it because as he did, he could see it transform in front of his eyes. It would appear to be quiet and still, but the longer he stared, he was able to see the life teeming within. Insects were flitting across the surface, tadpoles and minnows were swimming in the shallow waters, and fish were popping to the surface every now and then.

He looked up and spotted a couple of small turtles sunning themselves on a log across the lake. They had their heads high and their back legs sticking straight out behind them. He quietly laughed at their funny posture, and his eyes continued to roam upward to the bank across the lake. To the right of the turtles, Jim could see a squirrel moving quickly around a tree trunk, searching for things to eat and who knows what else.

As Jim watched the frenetic movements of the squirrel, a slight movement to the left of it caught his eye. His eyes flicked to the movement, but he saw nothing. Going back to the squirrel, he noticed that it was now standing stock-still, as if frozen in place.

Again, he perceived a slight movement.

This time, Jim began a methodical search of the area, but again he came up with nothing. He decided to keep his eyes on the spot that he thought had produced the movement. It happened again—some sort of movement, but it was difficult to figure out what it was. It looked like a tree was moving, but not like trees normally move. The whole trunk was moving.

It took Jim more time than he would be willing to admit to realize that it was not a tree. Unless trees take steps and can move laterally.

This was his bigfoot.

Jim's breath caught in his chest, and he quickly looked behind himself. John was staring at him with an odd, puzzled expression.

Jim quickly got up and walked over to the boys.

"Hey, can I have a try? The lake's boring today. No snakes or anything moving around."

"Sure," Dave said.

To Jim's dismay, John had not been deterred. He was still looking across the lake. Jim took a few shots that were very well placed and elicited a whoop from Sam. Stealing a look at John again, Jim saw him shake his head and turn back to the group.

"I think you have a tree down on your side of the lake," John said. "Saw it fall over or somethin'," he added.

Jim breathed a sigh of relief. He wanted nothing more than to run out of there right now and go see if he could spot the bigfoot again. Now would have been perfect since he knew where it was. Instead, he was forced to have lunch with the Whittles.

When Tess finally called them in for pizza, they entered the house to find Karen still there and looking just about as caged as Jim felt. Jim almost burst out laughing, and Karen gave him a warning look. It took another half hour to break free by using Jim's leg as an excuse.

When they were safely driving away, Karen burst out with, "That woman! She has this way of keeping you there. I just couldn't get away. It's like I was stuck in some sort of dream, where I couldn't escape."

Jim laughed at his mom.

She asked, "How was your visit?"

"Eh."

"Eh?"

"Eh. Dave's getting annoying. The other guys are okay, but they're just so into soldier stuff. It would be cool if they weren't so … *into* it."

"Are they planning to enter the Army or something?"

"Probably. That's scary. They really aren't that smart."

Karen laughed a loud, musical sound that always warmed Jim. He felt grown-up whenever he made his parents laugh.

The drive home was short, and Jim hopped out of the car as quickly as possible. He rushed through the door, straight through the house to the back door, and out onto the deck. Standing still, he surveyed the tree line to his left for any trace of the bigfoot. Seeing nothing, he headed for the steps.

When he got to the bottom step, he paused. For some reason, he wanted to see this creature again, but he had not really taken the time to think about why and if it was actually a good idea. Now that he was about to step into the woods again, he wasn't quite so sure about what he was doing.

Thinking about his first encounter, he felt very sure that if it had meant him harm, it definitely could have harmed him then, but it hadn't. He turned around and walked back up the steps, thinking. He wanted to take Banjo, but figured that the dog might scare the bigfoot away or cause problems. Unsure of what to do, he just stood there until Jilly poked her head out the door.

"What's up, Jimmy?"

"Hey, how was Sara's?"

"Fun! We got to play with her new Slip N' Slide. She doesn't have a pool, but that was fun." She came out skipping. "Want to go for a walk?"

Jim hesitated. He had decided that he wanted to go, but alone. This was unexpected, but he figured a short walk would be fine.

They set out across the yard, talking and looking at things. Jilly found a blackberry patch on the far side of the wood pile, and they spent a good deal of time picking blackberries and putting them in large cups that Jilly had retrieved from the house. This was always fun and always ended up leading to a delicious dessert. Jim's favorite was blackberry cobbler.

With cups filled to the brim, they started walking back up to the house. Jilly was practically running to show Karen how many they had picked. Jim was taking it slower to keep his leg from bothering him.

As he was walking, his eyes traveled over the woods to the right. Instinctively, he knew something was different. Looking back to the right, he saw nothing unusual, but his brain was still screaming that something was out of order. He scanned the area again with no change. A third, slow scan and he saw it.

Thirty feet away, there was a massive reddish-brown shape that resembled a tree. If he hadn't been consciously looking for that image, he probably would have dismissed it as a tree. Certain as he was standing there, Jim knew that it was the bigfoot. It was watching him. Apparently sensing that it was caught, it crouched down slightly and made eye contact with Jim.

Jim's spine tingled again, and he had a sudden urge to run, but he didn't. His instinct was to flee, but something else was telling him to stay. They stood there, staring at each other for what seemed like minutes until Jilly slammed the back door shut. The bigfoot looked curiously over toward the house and then back to Jim. It was no longer hiding from him.

The bigfoot raised up again and suddenly seemed to be melting into the woods behind. It moved so smoothly and effortlessly that Jim hardly noticed that it was backing away until it was nearly gone. Then it was gone with no trace that it had ever been there.

CHAPTER SEVEN
Close Encounter

THE NEXT DAY, Jim was out bright and early. His leg was feeling much better, and his limp was very slight. The swelling had gone down considerably, but his knee and ankle were turning a green color. Jilly thought the wounds made him look like a tough guy.

Jim walked the length of his backyard and found the entrance to the back trail. He felt no fear and was somehow sure that the bigfoot would not harm him.

Walking lightly and with his senses on high alert, Jim began his trek. He could hear birds in the treetops whistling and hopping from branch to branch. Going at an ambling pace, Jim was strangely at ease.

He was pondering that fact when a noise ahead of him stopped him in his tracks. Eyes unblinking and ears straining, Jim was prepared for an encounter with the bigfoot when a rabbit hopped into the trail ahead of him. He had forgotten how much noise even small animals can make.

Laughing at himself, he continued down the path, scaring the rabbit off on a small game trail toward the lake. He was still watching it make its way through the high grass as he walked.

When the rabbit ran out of sight, he turned and was stunned by what he saw in front of him.

The bigfoot stood—not ten feet away—quietly staring at him.

Now that Jim was right-side-up and on the ground, he could truly appreciate the massive size and quiet strength of the creature.

A pain in his right leg forced him to realize that he had frozen mid-step with all of his weight on his injured leg. A small gasp of pain escaped from Jim, making the bigfoot jump slightly. It looked down at his leg.

Jim noticed that its hair was damp, and it didn't seem to smell as strongly as it had before. If Jim didn't know any better, he would have thought that the creature had just stepped out of a shower. Maybe that's what it did in the lake, Jim thought. It must cool off in the water. After all, the summer heat was quite intense. Jim also noticed it was male.

The bigfoot sniffed loudly, taking in Jim's scent like an animal. They stared and surveyed each other. The bigfoot's eyes stopped on Jim's leg again. It met Jim's eyes and pointed. Jim's mouth dropped open in shock. It was communicating with him. Not sure what it wanted, Jim looked from his leg to the creature and back again.

"My leg? I don't know what you mean, but it's okay," he said.

Jim immediately wished that he knew sign language, but quickly realized that he was being stupid because the bigfoot would most likely not know sign language.

It stared at him and his mouth as he formed the words and then just looked at Jim again. Trying again, Jim reached down and patted his knee, then his ankle and nodded his head in what he hoped was a positive way. He was trying to convey that it was okay, but this was hard. Jim never knew just how precious words were until now.

The bigfoot seemed to understand and the concern that had been etched in its face seemed to lessen. Jim realized it was actually concerned!

It broke eye contact and looked from left to right, taking in the sights of the woods surrounding them. It was holding its hands together in front of itself and rocking slightly from side to side as it sniffed at the scents in the air and took in the forest. Jim was reminded of Jilly when she's nervous and indecisive.

Looking back at Jim, it turned and motioned with its massive, hairy shoulder for him to follow. It then took off with large strides into the woods. Despite its size, it moved with very little noise.

Somewhat in shock, Jim wasn't sure what to do. He hesitated for only a second and then moved to follow. Walking several feet behind the bigfoot, Jim studied its broad back. It was at least twice the width of an average man and, despite all the thick hair covering almost all of its body, Jim could see that every bit of it was well muscled. What was strange to Jim was that it had a definite ape-like appearance in most ways, but it moved with the athleticism and grace of a professional athlete.

They walked for only a few minutes, and Jim knew he was close to where barbed wire separated his property from his neighbor's at the very deepest and most secluded part of their land. The bushes became thick, and thorns were constantly trying to catch Jim's clothing and skin. They finally broke through these, and Jim found himself looking at a circle of trees that were hidden among a thick growth of yaupon shrubs. Yaupons were bushes that had small leaves and many red berries. The bigfoot turned and looked at Jim and then crouched down and entered the shrubs.

Jim could barely see it through the leaves, but this was where the bigfoot apparently slept. It had made a sort of nest in the middle of the trees and bushes. The bigfoot reappeared, holding something in its soccer ball-sized hands. It slowly walked toward Jim, breaking through the ten-foot barrier they had been keeping between them.

As it approached, Jim could see its face more clearly. It had leathery brown skin with a high forehead and thin lips that resembled those of an ape. As it came even closer, Jim thought he could see a youthful appearance. Somehow it reminded Jim of a young adult. Its face was fairly smooth, and its eyes had a look of wonder and curiosity that he associated with young people. It also seemed tentative and nervous.

Its hands were made of the same leathery skin and had thick, discolored nails. Both its hands and feet were enormously dispro-portionate to its height. This was another reason Jim thought it was fairly young. He remembered when Banjo was a puppy, and they had watched his paws grow well before the rest of his body had caught up.

In its hands were Jim's things that he had brought with him to the tree the day that he had fallen. He hadn't even thought of his pack until this very moment! The bigfoot had gone back and taken his pack after Jim and Karen had left. The items were loose in one hand and the pack was in the other. Obviously, the bigfoot had been examining everything.

It pushed the items out toward Jim. Mouth gaping, Jim reached out his arms and took the items back. He looked at what was in his arms. The granola bar was still wrapped, but the apple was gone. The water bottle had been squeezed and the binoculars were out of their case. Turning the camera on, he saw that the big-foot had accidentally taken a picture of the ground and one of its own face. The look on its face was one of curiosity and concentra-tion. It had been tinkering with his things.

Jim looked back up at the bigfoot in awe. He had the idea to slowly sit on the ground where the grass and leaves had all been flattened smooth by the bigfoot's coming and going. Slowly, the bigfoot did the same and, after examining Jim's crossed legs, it crossed its legs as well. They were now the two unlikeliest com-panions in the woods.

Taking the camera, Jim turned it around so the bigfoot could see the viewing screen. It reached out and looked at its own face on the screen. Jumping slightly, it gasped and then began looking from the screen to Jim's face, as if asking for an explanation. Jim had no idea where to begin explaining the process of photography.

Sudden inspiration struck, and Jim tentatively reached for the camera. It passed the camera back to Jim and waited expectantly.

"See, you push this button here," he said, pointing. "You aim the camera like this and push the button like this, and it makes a copy of the image you're looking at so that you can keep it. Like that. See?" Jim pointed the camera at a nearby yellow flower, snapped a quick picture, and showed it to the bigfoot.

The bigfoot scrunched up its face, looking from the screen to the flower and back again. Holding the camera in its large hand, it placed it beside the flower. With its other hand, it slowly grabbed the flower. Seeing the image of the flower and the real thing side by side, it let out a whoop of delight and bounced up and down on its butt in a celebratory fashion.

Jim laughed.

They repeated this process many more times, taking pictures of plants, a butterfly, and themselves. Each time seemed to delight the creature just as much as the first. Jim decided to move on to the binoculars. He picked them up and showed the bigfoot how to adjust them and to put them up to its eyes. This got another round of hoots and hollers. They even stepped out of their secluded spot to look at things farther away.

Jim grabbed his water to get a quick sip and realized that the bigfoot was staring at the process. Of course, it had no idea what the bottled water was. Jim took a few swigs to quench his thirst and passed the bottle to the bigfoot. It held it at eye level and studied it for a few seconds. Then it poured a small amount into its hand. It smiled and took a small sip. The crisp, clean water received the biggest whoop yet. It loved it!

Not wanting the fun to end, Jim opened his leftover granola bar. He thought this would be interesting for the bigfoot to try. He opened the wrapper while the bigfoot studied his every move and then broke the bar in half and took a large bite out of one piece. He then passed the other half to the bigfoot, who was no longer tentative about trying the things Jim showed him.

It took a relatively small bite with its horse-sized, square, yellow teeth and chewed thoughtfully. Its faced scrunched up at first, but with more chewing, it broke into a grin and it threw the remaining granola bar into its mouth.

Jim was having an unbelievable time with this creature. He decided that he should give it some sort of name instead of thinking of it as "Bigfoot."

"I want to give you a proper name." He pointed at himself and said, "I'm Jim. *Jim.*"

The bigfoot looked confused, so Jim repeated this several more times. On the last time, as Jim said his own name, the bigfoot pointed at him. Amazingly, it seemed to be catching on.

"Hmm. What should you be called? How about Yeti? No, that's stupid. And I should call you something that I can say in front of anyone, and they won't suspect what you are."

The bigfoot kept staring at his mouth as he spoke. This reminded Jim of his aunt's large parrot. She was a macaw that could talk. When Jim was trying to teach her new words, she would stare at his mouth while he said things and listen very intently. Eventually, she would start trying to say them. After a little while, she could repeat them.

Looking at this creature, Jim's mind went to how it had come into being. Was it some sort of missing link? Was it something that was only thought to have been extinct? Is it some newly evolved creature? Jim suddenly thought of Charles Darwin and his theory of evolution. He wondered what Darwin would say about this creature sitting before him.

"That's it! I'll call you Charles! No—Charlie!" He started pointing at Charlie. "You're Charlie. I'm Jim. You, Charlie. Okay?"

Charlie began following Jim's pointing and quickly learned to point to himself when Jim said Charlie. This was amazing.

A vibration in Jim's pocket alerted him to a text. Looking at his phone, he was shocked to see that it had been over an hour. Karen wanted him back at the house.

Standing up, Jim tried to mime that he was leaving and that he would be back. He pointed at himself and toward his house, and he then pointed at himself and back at the ground where they stood and shrugged his shoulders in a question.

Charlie looked puzzled. He wasn't getting it.

This went on for several more minutes and Jim began inching backwards, but Charlie was following. Jim kept walking, and Charlie kept walking. They walked quietly all the way to the back trail's entrance to Jim's backyard. Charlie stopped several feet from the tree line and just stood, staring. Jim pointed at himself and up to his house and tried to mime that he would sleep. He pointed at himself and then to Charlie and then back to where Charlie lived. Charlie seemed to understand now and gave a slight nod. He was already learning to nod for "yes."

Jim smiled, waved, and then turned around and trudged back up to the house. Turning back, he saw Charlie still standing there watching from behind a tree. Charlie waved, which made Jim break out into the biggest smile of his life. He was communicating with Charlie, and Charlie was learning very fast.

When Jim entered his back door, Banjo jumped on him, smelling him frantically.

"Banjo! Down! It's okay!"

"Where have you been?" Karen was watching the spectacle while cutting onions for dinner. They were going to have one of Jim's favorites: roast. "See anything good?"

"I was just walking around. I, uh, I saw a snake and some other stuff. It's cool out there."

"You were out there for a long time."

She had stopped and was now looking at Jim. It seemed like she knew he wasn't telling her everything. He hated lying to his mom, but this was something unusual. She would freak out. He couldn't tell her *this*. At least not yet.

"Yeah. I think I'm going to try to build a kind of fort. On the main trail. What do you think?"

He had always wanted to build a tree house or fort and thought this might be a way to spend a lot of time out there with Charlie without being too suspicious.

"That's a fun idea! You should ask your dad for help. He would love to help with that. I could bring you sandwiches and stuff. What do you think?" She was raising her eyebrows.

Jim smiled despite the ache in his stomach from lying to Karen. He lessened the feeling, but only slightly, by telling himself that he hadn't exactly lied directly—he just hadn't told the whole truth.

Still feeling guilty, Jim limped up the stairs to get cleaned up. When he reached the top, he saw Jilly sitting in her room.

"Jimmy! Where have you been? I've been wanting to play or something." She looked sad and pouty.

He felt a twinge of guilt for leaving Jilly out, but it hadn't been that long.

"What do you want to do?" he asked. "We can play hide and seek. I just want to shower first."

He ran and closed himself in the bathroom. He wanted some time to himself to think. Charlie was the most amazing thing to happen to him, and he wanted to savor his experience.

Later that evening, Jim was thoroughly exhausted from his most incredible morning and from playing with Jilly the rest of the day. At dinner, he felt like he was on a cloud. He was happy, excited, and very content.

"I saw a wolf on the way home from work today," Jack said. "Don't see those very often." He gave Jilly and Jim a wink.

"Ohhh! Was he big? Did he look mean?" Jilly was always making wolves and other predators male.

"He was huge! Bigger than any dog I've seen in a while. Bigger than Banjo. Sorry, boy," he added to Banjo, who was sitting beside him so very nicely and begging for food with his huge, round eyes. He always sat very straight, his head held regally high, thinking that this would earn him a treat.

This sort of thing normally would have excited Jim and elicited many questions and then a lecture on everything he knew about wolves. However, after the morning he had, Jim found the whole idea of spotting a wolf to be tame. Wolves can't compete with a real-life bigfoot.

As much as he wished to share his experience with his family, he kept quiet about it. Figuring he was being too quiet, though, he said, "Cool, Dad! Was it a dark one? You know that red wolves are now thought to actually be a hybrid between wolves and coyotes instead of a distinct species."

As usual, his family was staring in awe at his information. He usually had some sort of tidbit about most things.

"That's fascinating," Jack said. "I can certainly see that with all of the coyotes we have here."

It was true; they often heard coyotes howling at night. They would yip and howl and make all sorts of creepy sounds.

Jack continued, "Tomorrow's Saturday. Why don't we all take a boat ride or go for a hike through the woods? Jim, you can show us where all your excitement took place and where you want to build your fort."

Jim's stomach tightened. He had really wanted to visit Charlie tomorrow, but he had forgotten that Jack would be home. This meant he would have to wait at least a couple of days before he could see him again, and he had promised Charlie he would be back. Jim forced himself to smile and look enthusiastic about Jack's plans.

CHAPTER EIGHT
Weekend Troubles

THE NEXT DAY, Jim woke up feeling conflicted. He really loved it when Jack was home and they could spend the day outside, but he really wanted to see Charlie. He dressed slowly and headed downstairs.

Jack was at the kitchen table, reading a book. This was how Jim usually found Jack in the mornings.

"Hey, Dad."

"Hey. Your sister up yet?"

"Nope."

Jack got up and called up the stairs to Jilly. Jim poured some cereal and sat quietly, waking up and thinking. He hoped that Charlie would stay and wait for him again. Who knows how long a bigfoot stays in one place. Where did he come from?

After a tough time of waking Jilly, who loved sleep more than dressing up her cats, Jim, Jack, and Jilly cut through the backyard to the lake. They had a couple of fishing poles and a tackle box and were heading out on the water to see what kind of fish were out there. Usually they caught perch and some small bass. Sometimes they caught catfish with those weird, long whisker-looking things.

Jilly liked the small perch because they were "cute and small with pretty colors."

They pushed the family's small jon boat into the water from where it sat on the edge of the lake. Jilly jumped in and scrambled to the front. Jim followed and sat himself in the middle seat. Jack pushed them into the water and then hopped in. Jim and Jack began a slow paddle out to the middle of the lake, turned, and followed along their property line.

It was going to be a very hot day, and the morning was already sticky and uncomfortable. None of them really noticed, though, because they enjoyed this type of day. It was a lazy day, and Jim was having fun keeping rhythm with Jack as they paddled to a shaded spot where they had had success in the past. Jilly was using a stick she had found in the bottom of the boat to draw designs in the water as they glided along.

"Look, Jilly, an alligator!" Jim had spotted the eyes and nostrils of a small gator submerged in the weeds along the side of the lake. As they passed, it began a slow pursuit. This gator had followed them many times before, and Jilly called it Allington. She added "ington" to most of her names.

"Allington! He wants our fish." She was squinting back at him with her tongue clenched between her teeth. "He looks a little bigger."

They had now traveled to the end of the lake where their property met with their neighbor's property on the far side of their acreage. This neighbor, Mr. Black, had put up a fence that ran perpendicular to the lake and cut across it, separating his property from everyone else. This fence ran the whole length of the Thomas property and ended in the gate at the end of their front road. It was the most quiet here. There were plenty of trees that hung over the lake and provided shade. On a hot summer day, this was where the fish would be.

They set up to fish for a little while. Jack got their lures ready and handed Jim his pole. Quiet settled on the group as everyone got lost in their own thoughts.

Jim found his thoughts turning to Charlie. He wondered what he ate and where he got his water. Did he have any family? Were there others like him? There had to be others. How had he come to live here? Was he staying? Jim found himself trying to figure out ways to ask Charlie these questions.

"Jim! You have something!" Jack yelled.

He hadn't noticed that as he was automatically reeling his lure in, he had hooked something. He immediately began his series of reeling and letting it go slightly, then pulling back and beginning to reel again, just like Jack had taught him. It was a short battle of tug-of-war, but Jim won.

"It's so pretty! It's a big one, too! What a piggy!" Jilly was admiring his catch.

It was a fat perch. Jack got a nice picture of Jim holding it up and then Jilly holding it with a huge grin on her little face. He then helped pull the lure out of the fish and let Jim release it back into the lake.

Jim felt good.

He arched his back to stretch since he had been sitting hunched over for some time now. Sitting in the tranquil setting was making Jim feel a bit groggy. He felt like he could nap out here. Taking a deep breath, he looked around at his surroundings and took in the majesty of the woods. It was calming. As he scanned the woods across the water, movement caught his eye. It was almost imperceptible, but it was there.

His eyes shot back to where he had seen the movement—and there was Charlie. He was standing still in front of a large tree and practically invisible, but Jim knew what to look for. Charlie moved his right hand slightly, and Jim had the sudden urge to wave back, but quickly realized that would draw Jack's and Jilly's attention.

Suddenly full of energy, Jim felt happy knowing that Charlie was there watching them. Although he hated keeping secrets, he was thrilled to have this one.

They had fished for a good hour and were now making their way back to their pier. No longer forced to be quiet, Jilly was singing some silly made-up song about Allington and playing with a small beetle that was on the seat beside her.

"You guys want to have lunch and then go see what's out in the woods? Never know what you might find out there!" Jack gave them a little wink.

If only he knew, Jim thought.

"Sure!" Jim said. Jilly agreed as she hopped daintily out of the boat.

They returned to the house for a quick lunch of sandwiches and chips. Karen had the food prepared, and she had picked some wild flowers and put them in a small vase on the kitchen table. Lunch was spent regaling her with their stories of the morning and showing her the pictures of Jim's fish. It had been the only one they caught that morning, but it was still a success in their book. She gave the appropriate *oohs* and *aahs* and made a great listener for their adventure stories.

"Well that sounds like a great morning." She looked at each of them. "What's next for the day?"

"We're going for a hike!" Jilly exclaimed. "You should come!"

"That sounds fun. I think I will! Jim, I got your camera ready, so we can take it and get some pictures out there. Is that okay? Ours is broken, remember?"

Jim froze. He hadn't yet removed the picture of the bigfoot. Obviously, she hadn't seen it, but he didn't want anyone to turn it on and view the pictures.

His mind started working fast.

"Sure. I'll carry it."

"I've already packed it in my bag, but since it's yours, of course you can carry it."

She pulled it out and passed it over Jilly's head to Jim.

Jilly grabbed it.

"I want to look at Jim's pictures! He always has good pictures."

Jim grabbed it so quickly that everyone stopped to look at him.

"Here. I'll show you." He forced a smile at Jilly.

Not wanting to delete the picture of Charlie, he quickly skipped past it and found a batch of pictures he could show Jilly. They sat and looked at the pictures while their parents got ready for the hike. Jim finally breathed a sigh of relief when Jilly ran off to get a hat before heading out.

This hike was not as adventure-filled as the past few hikes, but Jim had fun with his family. He loved having his dad there. They both took the lead and were talking about different things and pointing out different animals or tracks to Karen and Jilly.

Karen had packed some water and snacks for them to eat, so they pulled them out and sat on some tree stumps to rest. They spent some time telling funny stories that they all knew so well but still loved to hear.

They all laughed particularly hard when Jim shared the story about how Jack had fallen into the pool fully clothed on a chilly fall day when he was trying to fish out a turtle that had slipped into the pool. He had yelped so loudly that birds had taken flight all around them.

Jim suddenly felt guilty because he had forgotten about Charlie for a short time. He looked around, hoping to catch sight of his new friend, but saw nothing unusual. Slightly disappointed, Jim turned back to his family.

As he did so, he heard a distinctive whooping sound. Charlie was making his whooping call for some reason. Jim glanced around and noticed that his family had frozen.

"What was that, Jack?" Karen was looking to her husband to explain the strange sound, but he looked just as confused as she did.

"I'm not sure. Maybe the Blacks are out clearing some trees?"

He was guessing that their neighbors were creating such an odd sound, just as Jim had guessed the Whittles were responsible when he had first heard it.

They all seemed to be shaking it off when another sound reached their ears. It was that growling noise that Jim had heard the day that he had walked with Karen and Jilly. The day they saw the deer.

Jim was beginning to worry about Charlie. Could he be in trouble?

As soon as he thought this, an intense barking came from the part of the woods where Jim knew Charlie lived. It sounded like the neighbor's dogs had cornered something and by the sound of the whoop and the growling, it was Charlie.

The barking was that of dogs on the hunt. He had heard this type of barking before when the dogs had cornered a deer. The deer had jumped into the lake and swum across to escape the huge dogs. Jim was fearful for Charlie, but he knew Charlie could take care of himself. There was no way these dogs could take down massive Charlie.

Just then, the barking grew more excited, as if one of the dogs had decided to attack, and there was a growling sound. The barking from the other two dogs grew to a fever pitch. Suddenly, there was a yipping noise like one of the dogs was hurt and the barking changed. It was no longer that of a pack of dogs in control. It was more like dogs that were scared and on the run. He had heard this before, too.

The barks were coming closer. A crashing sound alerted the family to the dogs seconds before they came rushing through the woods and streaked by them on their way home. The big white dog was lagging slightly behind the other two and limping.

Jim knew Charlie had taught the dogs a lesson and he smiled.

"Looks like they bit off more than they could chew, huh? Must have been some pigs or something. If so, they're lucky to be alive," Jack said knowingly. He then told them of another neighbor who had lost a dog to wild pigs years ago.

"Those dogs are annoying and I *love* dogs," Jilly said.

They all burst out laughing. It was true—these dogs were annoying. They ran all over, causing trouble wherever they went. Only Jim knew just how lucky they really were.

The rest of the hike was free from anything unusual. When they got back, Jim went to his room to try to figure out a way to check on Charlie. He figured the dogs may have tried to bite him, and he may need some help. Running to the bathroom, he grabbed some first-aid supplies and threw them into his pack.

He went back downstairs and found his parents lounging on the twin couches in their living room. They both liked to nap on the weekends, and he knew that after their outing they would both be napping for a while. Jilly was on the floor, playing with a Play-Doh set contentedly.

"I'm going back outside to take some pictures. I'll be back in a bit."

"Okay, stay close," Karen said sleepily.

"Okay."

He felt guilty agreeing to this with no intention of staying close, but he felt he had no choice.

Heading out the back door, he made his way over to the tree line and walked down to the back trail. From there, he began a hard run to where he had met Charlie on the trail the day before. After a short time, he made it and skidded to a stop. Charlie wasn't there, but Jim realized that he wouldn't just be waiting there for him.

Jim began cutting through the woods to where he knew Charlie lived. He saw where the dogs had found Charlie because the dirt was all ripped up from the struggle. Jim's stomach tightened. He hadn't imagined a real struggle, but it looked like one had occurred.

"Charlie? It's me, Jim."

He was walking slowly so that he wouldn't scare Charlie, but he wanted to hurry. There was a rustling sound in the brush ahead of him, where he knew Charlie slept. He stopped. Charlie's head peeked out from his stand of yaupons, and he slowly emerged.

Jim walked forward to greet him.

"Are you okay?"

Scanning Charlie's body, he gasped when he saw blood. Charlie's arm had wounds on it from an apparent dog bite.

Charlie saw Jim looking at his arm and kind of shrugged him away, but Jim moved forward and put a tentative hand on his arm. The arm was thick, muscular, and the hair was softer than he thought it would be. He pulled Charlie's arm closer and studied the wounds. They were deep and ugly, but he felt that they would heal with care.

Jim looked up into Charlie's eyes and saw that Charlie was appreciative of his concern. He reached into his bag and pulled out some cotton swabs and water, which he used to wash the wounds. Charlie jumped slightly when Jim poured the water on his wounds, but he seemed to understand that Jim was trying to help. Jim did the best he could to clean the wounds, and he put antibacterial ointment on them. Figuring that the hair would get in the way of a bandage, he wrapped his arm in gauze and taped the end.

Charlie was fascinated with the process and the supplies.

When Jim was done, Charlie surveyed the final product and felt his arm with his other hand. He seemed pleased and let out a quiet grunt to indicate this. He reached out for Jim and patted him on the head. Jim smiled and returned the gesture, but on Charlie's arm since he was so tall.

Knowing he had little time, Jim gave Charlie the rest of the bottle of water, which Charlie grabbed happily. He had also brought another couple of packages of granola bars. Charlie took these as well, and Jim watched him begin to unwrap the first one. Charlie had remembered how to open them.

Looking up at Jim, Charlie smiled. He actually smiled!

"You're welcome," Jim said. "I have to go for now. I'll come back tomorrow."

Charlie just looked at Jim, so Jim began backing away. Charlie's face seemed to fall as he realized Jim was leaving, but he lifted his hand and waved. He was learning so fast! Jim waved and turned to leave.

Walking slowly back to the trail, Jim felt bad about leaving Charlie. He thought that Charlie must be very lonely, so he promised himself that he would see him again tomorrow. Once he hit the trail, he took off at a run back to the house. His knee and ankle were starting to hurt, but he was able to keep up a decent pace. By the time he arrived, he was limping again.

He climbed the stairs quickly and entered the back door. It was a good thing he had taken a short time with Charlie because his parents were up from their rest and starting dinner.

"Where were you?" Karen looked up from her ground beef to get his answer.

"I went to the swing."

They had a rope swing that hung from a tree a little ways down the back trail. It had a wooden seat, and they all couldn't help but take turns on it most times they passed it on the trail.

"Oh. I thought I told you to stay close. That's a bit far. Next time stay in the yard." She went back to preparing her meatloaf.

"Okay, Mom."

Jim felt that he had gotten off easy since he had really been talking to a bigfoot and all. He ran upstairs to replace the first-aid supplies and decided to deal with his camera. He wanted to make sure that nobody found his picture of Charlie, but he wanted to keep it for himself, so he hid it in a folder on his computer and cleared it off his camera.

Jim started looking through the pictures they had taken that day. It had been a fun day and there were some great pictures. He was clicking through the series when something caught his eye. He flipped back to the last one that showed Jim and Jilly, on either side of Jack, with huge smiles on their faces. Behind Jim's right shoulder was something only he would have noticed. There appeared to be a large reddish-brown thing beside a tree in the far distance. Charlie had been watching them. Jim felt sad that Charlie was alone and had to hide.

Jilly came running into his room, and Jim clicked to the next picture.

"Jimmy! You spend too much time alone these days." She looked at him very seriously with her huge hazel eyes.

He couldn't help but laugh.

"Oh really? Well maybe I'm working on a secret project," he teased.

"What kind of project? Can I help?" She began a little hop from foot to foot.

"Maybe you can. Can I trust you?"

He was mostly teasing, but couldn't help but think it might be fun to include her in his secret.

"Of course, Jimsy! You can always trust me."

"Okay … we'll see, then." He got up to head downstairs.

"Yay! Can we have a club name?"

Jim burst out laughing again. "A club name? It's not a club!"

"Sure it is! It's a secret club!" She looked very serious and hurt that he would laugh.

He put on his most serious face and looked her square in the eyes. "Of course. You're so right. We can work on a name, okay?"

"Yeah! It'll be good, too. You're president, and I'm vice president, okay?"

"Okay." He shook her little hand.

"Let's go down and see about dinner."

CHAPTER NINE
Jilly's Scare

THE NEXT DAY was full of fun again. Jack took Jim and Jilly out for a morning swim that lasted into the lunch hour. They were thoroughly exhausted by the time they headed back inside.

After lunch, Jack again took them outside, where he talked to them about different flowers and trees. He seemed to know something about everything and was always teaching them some interesting facts, but he never made it boring. Jim loved his dad and treasured this time with him. He hated it when he worked during the week.

Jim was finding it very difficult to find any time to sneak off and see Charlie. The time seemed to fly by, and before he knew it, they were getting ready for dinner. He felt terrible about breaking his promise to Charlie, but realized that Charlie didn't know what a promise was.

Jack made a small bonfire so they could sit out and make s'mores for dessert. Jim helped find wood and build the fire while Jilly and Karen gathered the supplies. This was one of Jim's favorite things to do. He loved sitting around in the summer with a fire and watching lightning bugs dance in the darkness around them.

He started thinking about Charlie again and felt like Charlie was nearby. Jim wished that his family could know Charlie and be okay with him. It would be so much fun to have him as part of the family. He imagined what Charlie would think, sitting around a fire like this and eating sweet, gooey s'mores.

Yes, he felt his presence close by.

They all got to sleep rather late that night, and Jim woke up late the next morning. It took him a moment to realize that today he was free to try to see Charlie. That thought propelled him out of bed and down the stairs. Jilly and Karen were in the kitchen making pancakes.

"So Jim and I are going to come up with a name for our club and it's going to be so much fun!"

She had apparently been telling their mother about the club Jim had promised to start with her. This might be a problem if Jilly expected him to spend a lot of time doing club-related duties, whatever those may be.

"Yeah, Jilly's vice president," he said with a grin.

"I already told Mom that!" She sat up very straight in her chair and looked very pleased with herself.

"Jilly thought it would be fun to go look for places to build your fort. You guys didn't get to do that with your dad over the weekend. We thought it could be your clubhouse."

"Yeah, sure. Sounds okay."

Jim hadn't counted on this, but he would find the time to see Charlie at some point. He was just going to have to get creative.

After pancakes, they got ready to set out. Jim was going to take Banjo this time. He put his harness on and grabbed his leash.

"Ready to go?"

"Ready!" Jilly had a large stick that she had found on their last hike and was using it as a walking stick. It was a broken branch that would probably fall apart fairly soon.

They spent some time walking around, looking at trees. Banjo had fun running around and sniffing everything in sight. He got on the trail of some small animal and nearly dragged Jim into some large bushes, but Jim finally called him back. Jim liked watching his smiling dog have fun like this.

He briefly wondered what would happen if Banjo met Charlie. Would they get along?

Finally, they found the perfect tree. It was a large oak tree that was growing as if it was lying down with its top raised. There were plenty of branches all over to climb and a nice area where they could make a fort beneath the raised portion of the tree, against the huge trunk. It was in a good location at the intersection of the water well trail and the main trail that ran through the rest of the woods. Jilly was dancing around the tree, making suggestions here and there and singing with delight.

Having found their tree, they hurried back to the house. Jilly wanted to eat and get ready to swim anyway. Jim got a moment of inspiration and decided to make a quick break for Charlie.

"Hey, while you eat and get ready to swim, I'll go back to the tree and take some measurements and pictures for the fort plans," he told her.

Jilly looked slightly hurt that he was leaving her out of such an important process, but she agreed since it took her a while to eat and get ready for things.

"Okay, Jim. But I get to help with everything else!"

"You got it."

He took off at a run and headed to the tree first. He was going to take measurements and pictures, but as quickly as he could so that it was only half of a lie. Flying through the whole thing, Jim finished in minutes and then ran straight back to Charlie's place.

"Charlie?" he called.

Jim moved toward the bushes where Charlie slept and called
out again, but Charlie didn't appear. He crouched down to look
inside and saw Charlie was gone. Inside the crowd of bushes were
the water bottles and granola wrappers Jim had given him. To his
shock, Jim saw that the water bottles were full of murky water.

Charlie refilled them!

Turning around, Jim figured he would walk the back trail and
see if Charlie showed up. He started up at a quick pace and called
out every several feet, but still no Charlie.

A shriek erupted behind Jim.

It had come from the area of the tree that Jim and Jilly had
picked for their fort. In a gut-wrenching moment, Jim realized it
was Jilly. He turned and started sprinting back down the trail to
where he had heard the shriek. A blood-curdling scream rang out,
making Jim pump his legs even faster. What was more terrifying
than Jilly's scream was the squealing sound he heard next.

Pigs.

Wild pigs could be deadly, especially if they had young. He
was terrified by what he might find.

As he ran, Jilly let out another scream. She seemed to be running as well because her screams were moving deeper into the
woods to Jim's right, away from the house. Time seemed to be
slowing, and Jim felt that he couldn't move fast enough. He was
running as fast as he could and hoping that he was running in the
right direction. He anticipated where she might be now and pushed
harder.

Trees and bushes were flying by in a green blur. He could see
the fort tree ahead of him and used that to orient himself to where
Jilly might be. Turning to the right, in the direction of the Black's
land, he ran faster than he had ever run before. He jumped over
stumps, ducked under tree limbs, and shoved through thick stands
of bushes. Finally, he broke through the trees and into an opening,
just as he heard a menacing growl.

Jilly stood across from him with her back against a tree and her little white hands pressed hard against her face as she stared with huge eyes at the sight before her. The biggest pig Jim had ever seen was standing in the middle of the clearing, facing Charlie, who was to Jim's right. Jilly's eyes were flitting between the two.

The pig looked like a large boulder with ugly, yellowing tusks. It had black, wiry hair and a long snout. Jim was vaguely aware of a horrendous stench. This pig had to be close to three hundred pounds, and Jim noticed that it looked like babies had been nursing from it recently. It was a mother with babies—these were the most deadly.

Charlie began a sideways walk toward Jilly, trying to put himself between Jilly and the pig. This only seemed to further panic Jilly, who appeared to be having trouble figuring out which creature she should be more frightened of.

"Jilly, stay there!" Jim yelled to her.

This brought her eyes to him, and she took a step forward like she was going to run to him, but Charlie put out a large hand, and she flattened her back against the tree again.

The pig seemed to be scared of Charlie as well. It probably had never seen anything like him, but it also seemed to not want to back down. Jim watched it hesitate in place and then it sprang forward toward Charlie.

"No!" Jim cried.

He was afraid for Charlie, but Charlie roared and grabbed the pig with both hands. The pig flew into Charlie, and they rolled together away from Jilly. Jim's eyes were glued to the rolling beasts, and he ran forward to watch what was happening. He wished he could help Charlie, but there was nothing he could do.

Jilly suddenly crashed into him and clamped her arms around him so tightly he thought she would cut off his circulation.

"*Are you okay?*" he screamed at her. She nodded as she kept her eyes on the strange pair struggling in front of them.

Jim heard a horrible squealing sound and the pig was suddenly flying through the air. It hit the ground with a thud and a squeal, and ran off in the direction of the Black's property. Jim's eyes flew back to Charlie.

He was getting up from the ground and was rubbing his backside and the back of his head. Other than that, he seemed fine. Jim ran forward, which was difficult while he was encumbered by Jilly. He started looking for injuries on Charlie.

"Charlie! Are you okay?"

"*Charlie?* Jim, what is that?" Jilly was sounding hysterical. Her arms were even tighter than before.

"This is Charlie. He's my friend, and he saved me when I got stuck in the tree."

Charlie was standing there, staring at Jilly. He looked at Jim with an embarrassed, hesitant look on his face that Jim interpreted as his not knowing if he should leave or stay.

Jim grabbed Charlie's arm and looked deep into his eyes.

"Thank you, Charlie. Thank you for saving my sister."

Charlie smiled slightly. He looked at Jilly again, whose mouth was hanging open. She looked like she might faint.

"The pig chased me and then *he* came out of nowhere!" She was pointing at Charlie.

Jim made sure Charlie was okay and turned to Jilly. He bent down so that they were eye to eye.

"Jilly, this is Charlie. He saved me once and now he's saved you. He's a bigfoot."

Her eyes grew even bigger, if that was possible, and she gasped. Looking at Charlie, she seemed to realize that he was the thing she had seen that night.

"I knew it! I knew you existed!"

"Actually, you said it was a werewolf."

"Oh yeah. Well, I was sort of right!"

She looked at Charlie and then took a step toward him. Charlie looked unsure of himself and started wringing his hands. Jim had never seen Charlie look like this before. He looked vulnerable.

Jilly reached up and grabbed Charlie's right hand.

"Pleased to meet you, Charlie. Thank you for saving me." She looked so odd shaking a bigfoot's hand.

Charlie looked at Jim and back down at Jilly. He slowly smiled and even looked bashful, if Jim was reading him correctly. He reached out and petted Jilly's head with a surprising gentleness.

"Are we telling Mom and Dad about Charlie?" she asked.

"I don't think so. Not yet."

Jilly nodded in agreement. "This is our first club secret."

"That's right."

"I guess Mom didn't hear you screaming, but we should get back anyway. You have some scratches we should clean."

He had looked at her face and arms, which were covered in tiny red welts and scratches from thorns and branches clawing at her during her running escape.

"Charlie." He tried to gesture their intentions as he continued, "We have to go. We'll be back, though. Okay? Thanks for everything." He ended with a wave, which Charlie returned.

Jilly flung herself forward and hugged Charlie around the legs. Jim was surprised at how quickly she could be so comfortable with something like Charlie. Charlie looked stunned at first, but then reached down and put a hand on her shoulder. He seemed to like Jilly.

"Thanks, Charlie," she murmured into his hair.

"'Bye, Charlie," Jim said.

They started walking back, and Charlie walked with them. He was acting as their escort. When they had nearly reached the end of the water well trail, Charlie stopped behind a tree. They all waved to each other, and Charlie watched them climb the slight hill to their house and step onto the deck. Jilly and Jim turned, but Charlie was already hidden in the woods.

They looked at each other and broke into grins. Jim grabbed his sister and hugged her tightly for a few seconds. He rarely showed this type of affection, but he was so glad that she was okay. Jilly smiled brightly, and they went into the house.

Banjo assaulted them immediately with sniffing and licks. They had to fend him off and then found Karen in the living room watching TV while she folded clothes. She looked harried.

"Hey, you two. Jilly, were you out with your brother? You should always tell me if you're heading outside. I had no idea!"

Jilly turned pink and said, "I'm sorry, Mom. I wanted to help with the fort stuff."

"That's okay. Next time, let me know. Anything could have happened, and I wouldn't have known."

The two siblings shared a look.

"The washer's acting up. I had a load going and it went crazy making bumping noises. I couldn't get it to stop, so remind me to have your dad take a look at it when he gets home."

"Okay, Mom," they said simultaneously.

Without saying another word, they ran up the stairs to Jim's room. Jim knew that Jilly would want to know more about Charlie, so he ushered her inside and closed the door behind them.

Jim sat down in his computer chair and started from the beginning. He told her about the noises he heard, the prints and hair, and the horrible accident he had in the tree and how Charlie had appeared. He told her how Charlie had saved him. He then showed her the pictures, and Jilly giggled at Charlie's self-portrait. Finally, he told her everything he could remember about his meetings with Charlie and what they had done or said each visit. She was captivated and unusually quiet throughout the telling.

"This is amazing!" she cried. "Charlie's the bestest thing I've ever seen! I love him."

Jim laughed. "You just met him!"

"I loved Banjo and all of our kitties the first time I met them."

"He's not a pet!"

"I know, I know. But still. Do we count him as our brother now? How old is he? Where did he come from?" Her rapid-fire questions were making Jim's head spin.

"I don't know all of that yet. We can find out. But I think he's a fairly young version of a bigfoot. Don't you?"

"Yeah. I got that feeling too." She was staring at his picture on the computer screen.

Jim looked at his little sister. "Jilly, we can't tell Mom and Dad. Not yet. I want to know more about him and make sure he'll be okay. They would probably freak out."

"Okay, Jim. I'll do whatever you say."

CHAPTER TEN
Charlie's Story

THAT NIGHT AT dinner, the family discussed the new fort. Jack seemed excited to help them make a fort, and Jim wanted a good reason to spend time out in the woods. Not a word was said about Charlie or pigs. Jilly was keeping her word.

The next morning came quickly and brought thunder and lightning with it. A loud burst of thunder woke Jim up early enough that he was able to catch Jack as he was getting ready to walk out the door.

"Morning. You look grumpy," he said to Jim.

Jim was feeling grumpy. He had hoped that he and Jilly could go see Charlie and ask him questions.

"Hey, Dad. Be careful today." He plopped onto the couch.

"Always am! I'll see if I can stop by the store and get some supplies on my way home. If it isn't raining, of course."

"Hey, thanks!" This brightened Jim a little.

Jim watched Jack step outside onto the front porch and open an umbrella. He turned and gave Jim one last smile and closed the door. Jack worked really hard and always seemed happy in the mornings. Jim was not a morning person.

It rained all morning. Not just a little rain—it was a torrential downpour. Jim worried about Charlie in his little hiding place. He had begun to see him like a person instead of an animal of some sort. No person should be stuck outside in this, he thought.

Jilly was sitting on a chair in the living room and staring outside. He knew she was thinking about Charlie too, and probably hoped to catch sight of him somehow through the window. Jim remembered when he was like that just days ago and chuckled to himself.

They spent the morning helping Karen around the house and finding little things to pass the time. Jim wasn't interested in TV right now; he wanted to keep moving.

When the lunch hour rolled around, they helped make pizza, which was always fun because Karen provided a lot of toppings, and they got to choose what they put on their half of the pizzas. Jim was putting together a particularly complicated barbeque chicken pizza with a lot of vegetables, and Jilly was making an extreme-cheese pizza on her side. She had at least five kinds of cheese on it.

"That's a heart-attack pizza, Jilly," Jim teased.

"Shut up! Cheese is delicious!" She plopped even more cheese on top.

They popped their pizza into the oven and got some chocolate milk. Sitting by the kitchen window, they kept staring outside for long stretches at a time. When Karen stepped out of the kitchen for a minute, Jilly leaned in.

"Do you think he's okay?" Her brows were scrunched together with worry.

"He's probably fine. He's always lived outside. He's really tough."

Jim really wanted to believe what he was saying, but he was worried too. He couldn't imagine being outside in this.

"Yeah. You're right." Her brows smoothed slightly.

They munched on pizza while Karen worked around the house. She was always buzzing around.

While they were clearing away their plates, they suddenly realized the rain had stopped. It was still gray outside, but at least the rain had stopped falling. Jilly looked at Jim with the beginnings of a smile. He smiled back and turned to find Karen.

"Hey, Mom. Can Jilly and I go outside? There should be lots of puddles and streams to play in."

It was true. There were little trails of running water all over, and if enough time went by, with enough rain, puddles formed that became temporary homes to crayfish. Whenever there was a hard rain, the water found a way to rush down and through their land all the way to what they called "Blackjack Creek" in their backyard. It was a small natural drainage dip in the earth that, when full of rainwater, ran all the way from the water well trail, diagonally through their yard, and into the lake.

"Sure. Be careful!"

Right then, the phone rang. By the sound of things, it was their grandmother. This meant that Karen would be tied up for a while.

Putting on their rubber boots, they headed outside and began sloshing their way through the woods to find Charlie. Jilly had brought a bag with her, but wouldn't tell Jim what was inside.

It took them a few minutes to reach the back of the trail where they would need to veer off the path and into the woods. Jilly stayed close to Jim, and he could tell that she was apprehensive after her last venture into the woods alone. Every time they heard a twig break, she would spin her head to find the source of the sound.

Finally, they reached the stand of trees and bushes that housed Charlie. Jim stopped and Jilly bumped into the back of him. He somehow felt it would be rude to intrude any closer without announcing their presence. It was almost like knocking on some-one's door first.

"Charlie?" he asked.

Charlie peeked his head out of a small break in the bushes just as Jim spoke. Jim guessed that he had heard them coming and probably smelled them long before they got there. He slowly emerged from the bushes and looked pleased to see them. He was also sopping wet, but didn't quite seem to mind.

"You're all wet!" Jilly exclaimed.

She looked horrified to find him in such a sad state. She rushed forward and opened her bag. Making small noises that let Jim know this task was hard work, she slowly pulled a towel from her bag and shook it out with a triumphant grunt.

"Here." She presented it to him proudly.

Charlie reached out and took the towel, but didn't know what to do with it. He stood there, holding the towel and looking be-tween Jim and Jilly. He was slowly rubbing the material with his large fingers, but seemed utterly perplexed by the gift.

Jilly blinked for a moment and then realized what was happening.

"Oh! You don't know what a towel is. Here, let me show you."

Taking the towel, she began rubbing his arm down like a mom does to a child at the beach. She pulled the towel away and pointed to his arm.

"See? It's drier! Now you do it!"

She started miming that he should dry his other arm and his head. Pulling out a second towel, she motioned for him to bend down. Slowly, Charlie bent into a crouch and came eye to eye with little Jilly. She swooped the towel around his shoulders and pulled it tight around his thick neck.

Charlie seemed taken aback by the sweet gesture and just stared. Slowly, a small smile crept onto his face, and he looked away quickly. He put out a big hand and touched Jilly's small cheek and then stood up quickly.

Looking around, he pulled himself up to his full height and kept drying himself with his free towel. As he dried, he made little hooting sounds of joy.

Jim knew this was something he had never been able to do before, and Charlie was enjoying it thoroughly. He was reminded of a large ape that was figuring something out and of a person casually toweling off at a pool all at the same time. This was incredible.

"You doing okay, Charlie?" Jim asked.

Charlie looked at him with a smile. Turning around, he bent into his house again and came back out with some berries and leaves. He presented these to Jim and Jilly and then began eating some himself.

Jim had never eaten leaves or berries from these woods and knew the berries could make a person sick to their stomach. However, he didn't want to be rude, so he took some leaves and gave some to Jilly. He tried to smile in thanks and, taking a deep breath, took a bite of leaf. It tasted awful, but he chewed and swallowed a small amount. Jilly giggled and tried to do the same, but she wasn't as good at pretending.

Watching enthusiastically, Charlie hooted again when they ate the leaves. He was happy to be able to share something with them. Hoping that he had nothing else in his house for them to eat, Jim reached out and patted his arm.

"Charlie, do you have a family?"

As he asked, he pointed to Jilly and back to his house. Then he pointed to Charlie and raised his arms and eyebrows in what he hoped was a questioning way.

Charlie didn't seem to understand.

Looking around, Jim found a raised patch of ground with no grass or leaves covering the top. He grabbed a stick and walked over to it. Using the stick, Jim began to draw crude stick figures of himself, Jilly, and his parents. The ground was soft from the rain, so it was easy.

Pointing at the smallest figure, he said, "Jilly." He pointed at Jilly and repeated her name. Then, he repeated the gestures with the medium-sized figure and said, "Jim," while pointing at the figure and himself. He pointed back at the house and said, "Mom, Dad," while pointing at the larger figures. Circling them all, he said "Family." The female figures included hair and Jim pointed at the hair in the crude drawings and Jilly's hair. He hoped that Charlie was following because it seemed so simple yet so difficult to explain to a creature like this.

Drawing again, he made a larger figure and pointed at Charlie. Charlie pointed at himself and then the figure, and Jim nodded. Next, Jim pointed at the other figures that represented his family and raised his arms in a question again. He pointed at Charlie and at the figures and questioned again.

Charlie looked for a long time at Jim, then at the figures. Finally, he reached for Jim's stick. Jim and Jilly both held their breath as Charlie knelt down and began tracing figures. He deftly wielded the stick and copied Jim's stick figures to draw a slightly smaller figure, a slightly larger figure, and two even larger figures that had to be his parents.

Looking back up at Jim and Jilly expectantly, Charlie pointed at the second smallest figure and himself, then pointed at the smallest figure and at Jilly, then the slightly larger figure and held a hand a few inches above his own head, then pointed at each of the taller figures and held his hand at least a foot above his own head. He pointed at the larger figures and then at Jim's parental figures and looked at them with sad eyes.

So Charlie seemed to have a little sister, an older brother, and two parents.

Jim put a hand on Charlie's arm. "What happened to them?"

Charlie, clearly understanding that Jim wanted to know more about his family, took his stick and scratched out the figures of his parents. For his siblings, he drew trees around all three of them and then what Jim could only guess was fire. He drew three separate lines extending from each of the siblings and himself, running in different directions.

Finished with his story, Charlie looked at them.

"What does it mean, Jim? What happened to his family?"

Jilly's eyes were wet. She seemed to know that Charlie was upset and that something bad had happened.

"I think that his parents died and then there was a fire. He and his siblings were separated when they ran from the fire."

"Oh that's terrible!"

She gasped and looked like she was about to cry. Springing forward quickly, she wrapped herself around Charlie's neck. Charlie was surprised at this, but slowly put his long, hairy arms around Jilly, who almost disappeared in them.

Jilly finally pulled away with tears on her cheeks. Charlie looked at her and then stood. Jim stepped forward and put a hand on his arm to show his support. Charlie patted Jim on his shoulder. He then turned toward the path and started walking, so they followed. They had to take many scrambling footsteps for each of his giant strides, but they kept up.

Walking along in silence, they were lost in their own thoughts and enjoying each other's company. Charlie stopped here and there and sniffed the air; sometimes he bent down to look at tracks or plants.

Finally, they came to the lake across from a stretch of land where nobody lived. Charlie sat down and they sat on each side of him. For a while, they just stared out over the lake.

A buzzing came from Jim's pocket. It was a text from Karen letting them know that their dad was home. Jim turned to Jilly and filled her in. He looked at Charlie and said, "We have to go."

Charlie nodded. He was catching on.

Jim stood and tentatively approached Charlie. He leaned over and gave Charlie a hug around the shoulders. He felt the hefty weight of Charlie's arms encircle him, and they stayed like that for several seconds. Finally, he pulled away and Jilly latched on to Charlie from the other side. Charlie smiled and nodded, and they all stood. He walked them back to their house, where they all said goodbye.

With heavy hearts, Jim and Jilly walked slowly up the hill. They stopped at the deck and turned back, but Charlie was gone.

When they entered the house, they greeted their father and gushed over the supplies he had brought them. They listened politely while he told them his plan for their fort and then they had a pleasant dinner with their parents. The whole time, Charlie was in the back of Jim's mind. He was sure he was in Jilly's mind too.

As soon as dinner was over, they ran upstairs to Jim's room. Jilly wasted no time.

"Oh, poor Charlie!"

"I know. He's all alone right now. But think, there others like him out there."

"I wonder how many others besides his brothers or sisters or whatever."

"Me too."

"I wish there was something we could do for him."

"I think just being there with him is good enough."

"I hope so."

CHAPTER ELEVEN
Discovery

THE FOLLOWING AFTERNOON came quickly. Jim and Jilly spent the morning with Karen, doing house work and then swimming. The afternoon brought the first chance to see Charlie. Jim had been feeling guilty about not actually working on the fort, so he decided that he would take Charlie and Jilly to the tree, and they could visit while he worked.

Jim took Jilly down the trail to find Charlie, but when they reached his home, Charlie wasn't there. This had never happened, but Jim knew that Charlie wasn't always in his house anyway. They called out to him and slowly made their way back to their funny tree that looked as if it was lying down. Jim had brought a machete and sickle to clear away some of the greenery around the tree where their fort would be built.

He walked around and studied the area while Jilly climbed on the trunk that was lying sideways. She sat straddling the tree and making horse sounds, as if she was riding. Jim was looking at a couple of larger horizontal branches above the trunk in the spot where the trunk curved upward toward the sky. He thought this might make a fun deck or second story to their fort.

A squeal of delight interrupted his thinking, and he turned to find Charlie striding down the trail toward them. Jilly jumped off the tree and started dancing in place, eager to greet Charlie.

Charlie approached with a smile, obviously happy to see them. He gave a wave, and Jim said, "Hi, Charlie!" Charlie made a slight grunting noise in return.

Jilly walked forward, grabbed Charlie's hand, and pulled him over to the tree. She motioned for him to sit, and he looked at Jim for help, but Jim just laughed. Turning back to his work, Jim felt content with his life.

Jim was working on clearing a particularly difficult pile of branches and was only half-listening to Jilly babbling on and on to Charlie. She was telling him about her cats, about her family, about swimming, and everything in between. He could hear occasional giggles from Jilly and grunts from Charlie. After several long minutes, Jilly said, "Just a little bit more ..."

Curious, he turned around to see what they were doing. He was both amused and horrified by the sight before him. Charlie had bows in his hair and a toy cowboy hat that was large enough for Jilly, but several sizes too small for Charlie. He looked ridiculous, and he looked like he felt ridiculous.

"Jilly! How could you do that to him? He's a guy!"

"What? He looks so cute!"

She started fluffing more of his hair with a brush and turned around to bring out a bottle of something from her bag.

"What's that?" Jim asked wearily.

Charlie was now trying to follow their argument as they went back and forth.

"Perfume! So he smells nice."

"Absolutely not!"

Jim strode forward to take away the bottle, but Jilly got off a couple of sprays before he could grab it.

Charlie sniffed the air and started a big series of, "Ah, ah, ah, ah." The sneeze that followed was massive and made both Jilly and Jim duck for cover.

"Bless you!" Jilly said with another giggle.

She reached into her bag again and brought out a small mirror and turned it toward Charlie, who grabbed it eagerly. He looked into it for several long seconds, and his mouth slowly fell open. He began touching his face and head and then he felt the bows and the other changes Jilly had made.

Jim couldn't help but laugh. He laughed so hard it hurt and all three of them were soon laughing. Having never heard Charlie laugh before, it was a strange thing to experience. The laugh was more human-like than anything, but there was something ape-like in it, too. It was a deep, pleasant sound.

Charlie suddenly stopped mid-laugh and raised his head. He sniffed the air and stood quickly.

"What is it?" Jim asked. He looked around to see if he could see anything of concern and then tried to sniff the air himself. Nothing.

Charlie looked at him and pointed back at their house. He then waved and strode off into the thick woods.

"What happened?" Jilly asked. She looked hurt that he would walk off so suddenly.

"Where are you guys?"

They heard Jack's voice coming from the water well trail. Apparently, he was home early.

"Here, Dad!" Jim called. "We're at the tree!"

They could hear the crunching of twigs and leaves and swishing of bushes as Jack made his way to them.

"Hey! How's it going? Want to do some work?"

Jack was carrying some supplies he had bought for the fort. He had changed into older clothes and looked ready to work.

"Yeah!" Jilly yelled. Jim yelled his agreement.

He walked around, surveying Jim's work appreciatively. Many of Jack's weekends were spent outside working around the house, clearing the backyard, and maintaining the trails. Twenty-one acres of wild forest took a lot of work to maintain and Jack did it well.

"Looks good! You did some great clearing," Jack said with a proud smile. "Why don't we go over what you want it to look like?"

Jim gave what he thought to be a very professional proposal of what he would like while Jilly interjected with her ideas, such as a powder room for girls. Jack was impressed and gave some good suggestions. Since their plans were already fairly clear, they were able to begin some preliminary work.

Both Jim and Jilly kept popping their heads up to look for Charlie, but Charlie stayed hidden or he had gone home. After an hour, Karen delivered snacks and drinks and told them that she was getting dinner ready.

They decided to leave their work for the day and pick it back up tomorrow. They had a frame started that would make a nice square room beneath the trunk of the sideways tree and a platform started around the other side sitting over the trunk situated in the two branches Jim had noticed before.

Jim was thrilled about his fort. It was going to be very different from any fort he had seen, and he hoped that Charlie would be able to fit inside.

Walking back to the house, Jim couldn't help but look over his shoulder a few times, hoping to see Charlie, but he never did. Even so, he felt Charlie watching them. He always did these days.

After a delicious dinner of lasagna, made even more delicious by the hard work he had put in that day, Jim went upstairs to shower. He was so full that he was having trouble getting up the stairs. His mother's lasagna was his favorite, and he had overdone it, but he was satisfied.

He showered and headed back to his room to change. As he was putting on his shirt, his phone beeped the tone of an incoming text message. When he checked his phone, he saw he had three text messages and a voice mail. There was a missed call from Sam, and he saw that each Whittle boy had sent him a text.

Something had riled them up.

Quickly checking his texts, Jim's jaw dropped. They had seen something strange in Jim's woods from across the lake. Dave asked Jim if his dad was across the lake in some sort of camo, Sam said he saw a gorilla in the trees, and John said he had seen something strange weeks ago and thought that he had seen it again today. They wanted him to call them back as soon as possible.

Checking his voice mail, Jim got more information: "Dude! We were shooting when I looked up and saw something that looked like a stinkin' gorilla on your property! Dave says it was your dad in that crazy camo that snipers wear that looks like grass, but John says he saw it before, and he has no idea what it was. Have you seen anything lately? Call me back, bro!"

Jim's blood froze in his veins. This was the worst thing that could happen to Charlie. The Whittles were the last people who should see him. They would want to hunt him and mount him on their wall.

This was really bad. He had no idea what to do.

Pacing his room, he was trying to think of some excuse for what they saw. He couldn't tell them it was his dad because his dad wouldn't go along with it. Maybe he could keep them from talking to each other forever. But he knew that wouldn't really work.

He heard Jilly bounding up the stairs and shot out the bedroom door.

"Psst. Jilly! Come here."

She stopped and looked confused, but walked over, and he grabbed her arm to pull her in.

"This is bad, really bad. The Whittles saw Charlie, but they're not quite sure what they saw. But they saw him! I don't know what to do."

Jilly's hands shot up to her face with a gasp.

"Oh no! Charlie! We have to protect him. Lie to them. Do whatever you have to. I'll … I'll lie too."

She looked defiant. He felt like hugging his little sister. She didn't like lying either and for all he knew, she never had.

"Okay, I'll call him back, but I have to have a good explanation for what they saw. Let me think."

He could only think of one thing, but he was sure it wouldn't work if they ever talked to his parents. Hopefully, they wouldn't tell their parents because their parents would talk to his parents. Why did Charlie go near them? He could have gone to a more secluded part of the lake. Maybe he was getting complacent with humans now that he knew Jim and Jilly. Not everyone was like them, though. If anything ever happened to Charlie, Jim wouldn't forgive himself.

Somehow, he felt like this was his fault.

"Okay, I'm calling them. Shh."

Jilly sat on the edge of his bed. He stood up and continued to pace. The line started ringing.

"Hello?"

"Hey, Sam. It's Jim."

"Jim! Dude! Get my message? You won't believe what we saw!"

Sam sounded really excited. This was bad. Jim decided to play like he didn't know what Sam was talking about and see just how much they had seen.

"Yeah, I got your message. What did you see?"

"Oh wow. I'm looking down at the target, right? And I look up across the lake, and I see this big shape standing there. At first, I thought it was a tree, but then it moved! Can you believe it?"

"What was it?" Jim was squeezing his phone so hard he thought it would break.

"I have no clue, man. Dave swears it was your dad in that weird camo get-up the snipers wear that looks like grass, ya know? But John here, he thinks he may have seen something days ago and the same thing today. Whatever it was, we only saw it for a couple of seconds and then it seemed to dissolve into the background. It was awesome! You should have seen it! Heck, it was practically in your backyard! Go out and see if you can catch it!" He heard laughing from all three boys.

"That's insane. I bet it was another poacher."

He had thrown this out there as casually as he could and hoped they would buy it.

"A what? You say there was a poacher there?" Sam sounded slightly dejected.

"Yeah. Well, there was one weeks back. The guy was hunting on our back trail, and Dad went out and scared him off. Called the game warden and everything."

His story had really happened weeks ago. He had taken inspiration from a true event in the hopes of making it sound as realistic as possible. Also, he thought that if they knew his parents had known about the first poaching incident, the boys might assume that he would tell them about what they had supposedly seen. This might make them think the situation was taken care of and keep them from wanting to talk about it anymore.

"Ah, man," Sam said. "That sucks. I thought it was something cool. I bet you're right. What?" Jim knew he was now talking to his brothers. "Jim said they had a poacher out there weeks ago and that's probably what this was. Just some guy hunting on their land. Probably was wearing that crazy camo stuff because he got caught last time."

Jim was starting to feel like he could breathe again. His grip on the phone hadn't lessened yet, but he had slowed his pacing.

Jilly seemed to sense his mood change and was looking questioningly at him.

Sam was back.

"Okay, well that's probably what it was. Man, I wish it had been something cool. Thanks, Jim. Hey, want to come over tomorrow?"

Jim definitely didn't want to go over there now that they had seen Charlie, but he didn't want to act strangely, so he said he would. They agreed to meet at the corner of the road on their bikes at lunchtime the next day, and they hung up.

Jim breathed a huge sigh of relief, and Jilly jumped up.

"What happened, Jimmy?"

"It sounds like they bought it. At least Sam did."

"That was good thinking! It sounded real! You're a good liar!"

She was dancing around the room now. Jim laughed. He didn't like being a good liar, but this was a special circumstance.

"Okay, want to go watch some TV to celebrate?" he asked.

"Sure!"

CHAPTER TWELVE
The Whittles' Search

EARLY THE NEXT morning, the sun had moved enough to start streaming into Jim's open eyes as he lay in bed. He hadn't slept well and woke up early with his mind on Charlie and the Whittles. They just had to believe him, and he really needed to go see Charlie. He wanted to somehow warn him to stay away from that part of the lake.

When the hour seemed appropriate, he got up and went to wake Jilly. She jumped awake with her eyes heavily lidded.

"What? What's going on?" She was lying back down again as she said this. Usually, that meant she was already asleep.

"We're going to see Charlie. We have to tell him that he needs to stay away from the lake."

He grabbed her hands to pull her up again, but she was dead weight.

"Jilly, go back to sleep. I'll go find Charlie and tell him, okay?"

Snoring told him Jilly was already asleep.

Jim tried to descend the creaky stairs quietly and walked into the kitchen. Jack was there, drinking coffee. He hadn't left for work yet and looked surprised to see Jim.

"Morning. What's up?" He looked at Jim expectantly with eyebrows raised.

"I was going to go out and see the fort before I have to meet the Whittles. I think I left something out there, and I want to plan. Can I go really quick?"

Jack took a sip of coffee. "Be quick. I have to leave soon, and your mom's not up yet. Want me to come with you?" He started to stand, but Jim waved him back down.

"I'll be okay. You're already dressed for work. Thanks, though." He smiled and gave Jack a quick hug.

Banjo was asleep by the back door, and Jim stepped carefully so that he wouldn't wake him. His snores were so loud Jim imagined he could hear nothing over his own noise. Jim slid the door open and slipped outside.

The early morning air had that slightly cool and fresh feeling. There were birds chirping lightly and flitting around the trees. Jim took in the summer smells and stepped off the deck.

He hadn't been out in the woods this early in a long time. Everything was quiet and still. He pictured many of the animals still sleeping comfortably in their hiding places. There was a sense of calm, and Jim liked feeling like he had the woods to himself right now.

Walking quickly, Jim made it to Charlie's in short time and called out quietly. As he did so, Charlie stepped out from behind a tree to his left.

"Hey, Charlie! Morning! I need to talk to you." He marched forward.

Charlie greeted Jim warmly with a pat on the shoulder and walked to his little sleeping quarters. Bending down, he went inside the bushes where he slept and motioned for Jim to follow.

Crouching low, Jim entered the cozy space and sat down. Both he and Charlie were sitting comfortably with their backs against two trees under the cover of the yaupon bushes. The space seemed just the right size and the ground was dry and packed nicely. There was a padding of leaves for bedding, and some of the items Jim had given Charlie were set aside against another tree.

Oddly enough, Jilly's bows and hat were there, too. They looked so out of place.

"Charlie, you have to be careful and stay away from the lake. My neighbors saw you and they could make trouble for you. I would hate that."

He knew Charlie couldn't understand, but he had to try.

Leaning forward, he grabbed a twig and decided to try the method that had worked before. Digging it into the dirt, Jim drew what he hoped looked like the lake and trees to represent the forest where they were. He pointed at the lake and used his fingers to motion walking toward the lake. Pointing at Charlie while doing this, he said, "No," while shaking his head. He drew some stick-figure people on the other side of the lake and pointed to his eyes and then at Charlie and again shook his head.

Charlie seemed to be getting it because his eyes narrowed, and he looked back over his shoulder in the direction of the lake. Jim felt relief that Charlie was so smart and seemed to understand what felt like nonsense. Finally, Charlie nodded, and Jim hoped he really did understand and would stay away from the lake.

"Charlie, can you speak?"

Jim had been curious about this for a while. Charlie seemed to be able to understand them and it would be exciting if he could speak, but Jim wasn't sure how all of this worked. Was he capable of human speech?

"Jim," he said, pointing to himself. He began repeating it normally and then slowly. He motioned for Charlie to try. "Jim. Jiiiiimmm."

Charlie started moving his mouth as if trying to make the same movements as Jim. After a little while, Jim could hear him making small sounds. He started with a "J" sound. After a few tries, Jim thought he could hear a very crude "Jim" from Charlie. It was a very deep, animal-like sound, but it was definitely his name.

"Yes! You did it! Oh wow, this is great!"

His gray eyes dancing, Jim pumped his fist into the air in excitement. Charlie broke into a huge grin. Looking at his watch, Jim saw that he had been gone for long enough and needed to get back to Jack. He sighed and started to raise up.

"I have to go, Charlie."

Charlie seemed to be learning this phrase and the way Jim said it because he nodded his head, and they both started to crawl out of Charlie's hiding place. As they stood, Jim looked up at Charlie and wished that he could stay. Charlie was amazing and quickly becoming his best friend.

"'Bye, Charlie. I'll see you later." He waved goodbye, and Charlie returned the gesture.

Jim turned and headed back to the house. By the time he got back, Karen was awake and making breakfast. Jack was gathering up his things to leave.

"Hey, everything go okay?"

"Yeah, Dad. We'll have to talk about my ideas when you get home."

He watched Jack go out the door. Even though he was preoccupied with Charlie, he really loved having Jack work on a project with him.

Jim spent the morning trying to anticipate any problems with the Whittles. He paced his room with some music on, but he wasn't really listening. Sam had sounded like he believed Jim last night, but Jim wanted to be prepared. These were people he wasn't worried about lying to, but he wanted to avoid it if possible.

When Jilly woke, she popped into his room and, to Jim's surprise, was upset that he had left to see Charlie without her. He tried to reason with her, but she had that fiery temper that they say

comes with red hair. She stormed out of the bedroom, and he
didn't see her for the rest of the morning.

At noon, he went out to the garage to get his bike. It was a
prized possession of his. Even though he didn't take it mountain
biking, it was a really nice mountain bike that he got for his birthday last year. He really wanted to take it to one of those biking
trails and go crazy, but he hadn't yet. Still, the terrain around the
neighborhood could be pretty rough, so he got some good use out
of it.

Hopping on smoothly, he took off down the long, wooded
driveway to the road. Looking left, he could see the Whittles already gathered at the corner. They were meeting where the
Whittle's road and Jim's road met.

"Hey, Jim. How's it going? Any more poachers?" Dave's
question made Jim feel better about whether or not they believed
him. He wished they would leave it alone, though.

"Nope. Not that I know of. That was weird, huh?" He was
trying to be casual and thought he was doing a pretty good job.

"Yeah. Could have sworn it was some bigfoot thing or
something," said Sam.

Jim could hear the disappointment in Sam's voice and see it
on his face.

John nodded in agreement.

"What are we doing today?" He was hoping to get this over
with quickly. He liked doing things with them on occasion, but
now was not the time.

Sam and Dave looked at each other.

"Well, we were wondering if you would take us on your property, and we could look for signs," said Sam.

Jim's stomach clenched. "What signs?" he asked.

"Signs from the poachers. Or something else," Sam said. They
looked at Jim.

This was what he was afraid of. One or more of them didn't believe the poaching story and had convinced the others. Jim tried to take a deep breath without them noticing and look indifferent about the matter.

"Nah. There's nothing there. I looked. They didn't get anything, I guess. We never heard a shot this time. Last time, though, we heard it. It was a loud crack, and we knew right away what was happening. So my dad, he goes outside with his pistol on his hip. He walks down the driveway with a spotlight and shines it on their car. Next thing you know, they're speeding down the road out of here! It was great."

He had hoped his excited ramble would draw them into the story and away from their idea. He had completely ignored the "or something else" line.

John had perked up with his story and seemed like he was about to ask a question, but Sam jumped in with, "Well that's crazy, but I really do think I saw something weird and I think it would be cool to look around, ya know? What's the harm? Hey, maybe we'll find something that shows where the poacher guy went and what he did."

Jim didn't like this.

"That's crazy! You think you saw, what, a yeti or something? Come on, guys. This was some guy dressed up funny. He was trespassing and should be put in jail, but that's it. Besides, I don't think my parents want us messing around out there."

"Why not? Come on. We'll even ask your mom!" Dave was now in on it.

Jim was getting mad. He felt himself starting to twitch with anger, but was trying to control it.

"Let's just go to your house. There's nothing fun over at mine. We can play paintball on your course. Didn't you guys tell me you killed a pig a while back? I want to see where it happened."

He started to pedal his bike down their road and hoped that they would follow.

"Hey, Jim! We can do all that, but while we're here, let's just go talk to your mom and then take a look. We'll meet you back at your house!"

Dave was riding off while he yelled this, and his brothers began to follow. There was no way to keep them away without looking panicked and suspicious.

With no other recourse, Jim followed. They drove their bikes up the driveway and parked them behind Karen's Jeep.

"Hey, nice Jeep! New?" Sam was appreciating the car on the way up to the house and all Jim could do was follow.

"Sorta," he said.

His only hope was that Karen would object or that he could somehow silently communicate with her that he didn't want to do this.

They passed through the gate that led to the front door and found Karen on the front porch. She had just made a phone call and was standing up.

"Hey, guys. How are you?" she asked with a bright smile. She was always so warm to people, even the Whittles.

Dave took the lead.

"Hi, ma'am. We're fine. How are you?" he asked with extreme, and fake, politeness. The other two murmured something along the same lines.

"Doing just fine. What's up today?"

She glanced at Jim, but not long enough to see his discomfort.

"Well, Mrs. Thomas, we were talking to Jim and wanted to know if we could walk through your property a bit."

Thankfully, they didn't mention the non-existent poachers. Jim was trying to catch Karen's eye to shake his head "no" when she turned to head into the house. She wasn't looking in Jim's direction.

"Sure. That's fine, but stay together and be careful, okay?"

She was rushing into the house with something else obviously on her mind, so this was a disaster for Jim. He had no idea how Charlie would react and there was no way to warn him. A fleeting idea to send Jilly to Charlie before they could get there was quickly dismissed. She was too little for something like that.

The boys pedaled back down the driveway and turned right at the road. They rode along Jim's property until they reached the second drive that led to the back of the property. Here, they rode their bikes partway into the drive, where the trees grew wildly and provided some cover.

They left their bikes behind the cover of bushes and started walking down the trail. This trail would take them by the fort tree, by the turn-off for Charlie's place, and eventually out the back trail. It was all connected and there were smaller trails that led off in different places, but this was the main path.

As they walked, Jim was constantly swiveling his head, looking for Charlie. He was very tense and worried about what would happen if Charlie saw them or sensed them somehow. Would he come out to greet them? He hadn't really done that yet. He usually waited for them to call him.

"Does this go to the lake? That's where we saw it." Dave was leading and looked back at Jim, but didn't seem to be waiting for an answer.

"Yeah. What do you think you saw?"

Sam answered.

"I saw something tall and hairy. I know how that sounds." He had mistaken Jim's look of unease as skepticism.

"Yeah, I saw something like that a while back," John finally piped up. "That day you came over, and we were shooting the paintball guns. Then I saw it yesterday too. I only saw it for a second, and just part of it, but from what I saw it was big and hairy."

"And I could swear it was on two feet," Sam added. "Dave didn't really see it. Sort of out of the corner of his eye. He just watched this show on snipers, and he says what he saw was like that crazy camo get-up they wear in some places. You know, that looks like grass and stuff so they can lay themselves down and blend in?"

"Yeah. Hey, that makes sense," Jim agreed. "Especially if it's the same guy who trespassed before. He would have wanted to be invisible this time."

"But they were here in the day. The guy came at night before. You would think that if they were doing something illegal, they would come at night," Sam argued.

"Nah, see they would want to change things up. Maybe they thought my dad, and anyone else, would be at work during the day and it would be a better time. Right?" Jim asked.

All three of them stopped and looked at each other and then at Jim. Sam was the first to concede.

"Yeah. That actually does make sense." He looked at the ground and kicked at a rock.

"Well, I'm still going to look," Dave said with a defiant glare. Turning to his brothers, he said, "You guys are forgetting what we talked about last night. That makes sense and all, but it doesn't explain the footprints we found and the hair."

Jim went cold. That's how he had started believing in Charlie. He hadn't thought about that in days and now wished that they hadn't remembered.

"I thought you guys recognized them as cat prints and deer hair?" Jim asked. "That made sense. Remember, the simplest explanation is usually the correct explanation. It's Occam's razor."

"Occam's what now?" Sam was interested.

"A philosopher popularized the idea that simple explanations are best. He was William of Occam," Jim explained.

The three brothers looked at each other and back at Jim like he was an alien.

"Always comes up with crazy stuff, doesn't he?" John was smiling appreciatively.

"Thanks for the lesson, professor, but I think we'll still take a look around." Dave was already stalking off again.

They walked on. John and Sam were talking about how cool it would be to find either a poacher or a creature. Sam was leaning toward it being an ape, and John was leaning toward a bigfoot.

If the situation wasn't so serious, Jim might have laughed at how right they were.

Dave was walking quickly and stopped every now and then to take a dramatic look around. Jim couldn't figure out why he was being this way. If Dave was worried about being right, his first idea that it was a hunter in camo *was* right when looking at Jim's concocted story. He was always being stubborn and confrontational these days. Now that Jim had struck down their idea of it being anything else, Dave was determined to prove Jim wrong. Jim had the fleeting idea to start agreeing with them about it and trying some reverse psychology, but he was afraid that it would backfire, and they would just get more encouraged, so he stayed quiet.

As they walked along, the Whittles assumed quiet, intense personalities and walked as though they were trying to be soldiers. When Jim noticed that they were communicating using a series of hand signals, he almost burst out laughing, but somehow managed to rein it in.

This was an absolute nightmare for Jim. He was trying not to be noticeable as he searched the woods for signs of Charlie. When they reached the lake with no excitement, Jim started to feel like he could relax a little bit. They walked down a game trail to the edge of the lake and looked across to the Whittle's pier.

"Come on," Dave said as he turned left and started walking down the bank, away from Jim's house.

"Where are we going?"

Jim had assumed that Charlie had been spotted here or closer toward Jim's pier. In fact, he had been a little annoyed that Charlie had been so careless to have been seen from the Whittle's backyard.

"Down here. We were walking around the Clarke's place when we saw it."

Sam was in front of Jim. He had picked up a branch and was holding it like a rifle.

John was unusually quiet, and Jim took a look at him. He was smaller and younger than the rest of the group. Jim suddenly realized that he was scared. John was holding his hands together and fidgeting with them. His shoulders were slumped, which made him look even smaller than usual, and his eyes were wide and darting around. He was staying very close to Dave's back as they walked. Knowing his brothers, he was probably trying to stay quiet and keep their attention off the fact that he was scared. Jim felt bad for John.

Walking a little faster, Jim passed Sam, who was pretending to aim his branch at a passing hawk overhead. He caught up with John, who flinched when Jim's footstep broke a twig on the ground behind him. He swung around quickly and saw Jim, then averted his eyes. He looked like he thought that something was going to attack them at any moment.

Jim realized that John had probably gotten the best look at Charlie. John had seen him and knew what he was. That's why he was so scared.

He stepped up beside John and started walking by his left side instead of single-file as they had been. With Jim walking beside him, John started following Jim's pace. Jim slowed down and let

Dave get out of earshot. Looking back, Jim saw that Sam was still several steps behind and playing with his fake rifle.

"Hey, John."

John looked over at Jim, then beyond him to the woods.

"Hey." John looked back down at the ground.

"Nothing's out there, you know. Nothing that can hurt you," Jim said. The last part was true.

John didn't say anything. His eyes stayed focused on the ground in front of him, and he stiffened.

"It's not like some giant ape thing is out there." Jim tried to say it with a laugh and sound like he believed it.

John still said nothing. Finally, Jim heard a quiet, "It's not an ape."

Jim was now sure John had seen Charlie. The only thing that was saving them right now was that John didn't want to sound crazy to his older brothers.

Jim wasn't sure what to do. It would be normal to ask what it was, but he really didn't want to encourage it or to get him comfortable talking about it. Dave stopped suddenly ahead of them, saving Jim from having to say anything else.

"There's where we were."

Dave was pointing across the lake now. This part of the land belonged to the Clarkes, and the Whittles had clearly been trespassing when they had come upon Charlie.

In this rural area, it wasn't uncommon for people to explore or pass through a neighbor's property, but usually people tried to limit it to friends. The Clarkes were well-known for not liking trespassers and had stories about destruction of certain things on their property. Jim now had a hunch that the Whittles were responsible for these things.

Sam turned away from the lake and started looking through the woods. He seemed to be looking for something. "There's about where it was." He was pointing and then started walking through the woods.

Taking a winding path through bushes and around trees, the group finally stopped in a small clearing. Sam looked back and forth between the clearing and where the brothers had been standing across the lake. Satisfied, he looked at everyone and smiled. "This is it. Let's look around."

They began searching the surrounding area for anything un-usual. Jim was actually searching too, but only to obscure any pos-sible signs of Charlie. He was looking really hard and trying to be quick.

"Hey! Over here!"

It was Dave. He was standing by a tree about three feet into the brush outside of the clearing. Rushing over, they all bent to see what he was looking at. It was a very light indentation in the dirt. Jim could see that it was the ball of a foot, but the others didn't seem to know what they were seeing. They might have recognized that it was unusual, but nothing more. Luckily, the toes hadn't come out very well, so it wasn't very clear.

"What is it? It doesn't look like anything." Sam was screwing up his face as he tried to make sense of the indentation.

"It's a print of some sort! I don't know what it is, exactly," Dave replied testily.

John was standing very still and looked more worried than ever, but he said nothing.

Jim was thinking very quickly, but couldn't decide on what to do. He said, "I can't really see anything. Where are the toe pads?"

"I kinda see one or two toes, here and here ..." Dave was studying the prints again, but seemed to be having trouble figuring them out. "I swear it's a foot with toes, but the toes didn't come out."

"Sorry, bro. Looks like nothing to me," Sam said.

He was already moving on and didn't seem to have his heart into it. Ever since Jim had provided an alternative theory for everything, he seemed to have accepted that.

Jim kept stealing glances at John and trying to decipher his expression. He was hoping that John would keep quiet and eventually believe that he was wrong.

Another half-hour of searching brought nothing. Dave kept the speculation going, but Sam was already talking about what they would do when they left.

"We can ride over to that place over by the bridge. There are some trails we can ride on that are really cool. There's this one big hill that has like a ramp at the end, and you can get a huge jump there!"

"Yeah, I think we should go do that," John said quickly. He was wringing his hands and kept looking over his shoulders.

"That would be cool," Jim quickly agreed.

They all stopped and looked at Dave. He looked back at all of them with a scowl, but saw that he was defeated.

"All right. There's nothin' here. Looks like I was right in the first place. Y'all are idiots for thinking there was anything else out here. Just a hunter. Let's go." Dave's tune had changed rapidly with his defeat.

Jim breathed a sigh of relief and led the way out as quickly as he could. As they passed the fort tree, he was feeling like he had just managed to escape some real danger. He could now see the opening of the trail that led to the road. If they could all just stay with him for a little while longer, Charlie would be safe.

Just as he thought this, a roar sounded from behind and to their right. This was near where Charlie usually was. It sounded like Charlie was in danger. Jim's blood froze, both in fear for Charlie and fear that the Whittles would go looking for him.

All four boys were frozen in place for a few seconds and then the Whittles started looking around. Jim tried to assume a casual look and said, "Sounds like the pigs are going crazy."

"Pigs? I don't think so." Dave was looking as if he wanted to go back and check it out.

Sam said, "Maybe. Pigs make crazy sounds." He looked like he wanted to get out of there. John was already edging back toward the road.

"Yeah. Jilly almost got killed by a mother pig the other day. Did I tell you that? She got chased around by one," Jim said. He felt panicked and thought he was making too much eye contact in his attempt to distract them, but he couldn't help it.

"No way!" Sam's mouth was hanging open in awe. "She okay?"

"Yeah. She's tough. She got in some thick trees and it stopped."

"Should we go see if we can find what it was? Didn't sound like a pig to me." Dave was still trying to prove Jim wrong. He had his arms crossed over his chest.

"We could get hurt if there are pigs fighting or somethin'. Anyway, Mom wanted us to help with lunch, remember?" came John's timid voice. He was now twenty feet away and still backing toward the road.

"Oh fine," Dave said. He looked mad, but there was also some fear in his eyes. This was a good excuse for him to save face and leave.

Jim started walking toward John, and the others followed. Before long, they recovered their bikes and were riding back down the road. Jim had had enough for the day and really wanted to find out about Charlie.

"Hey, I really need to get home. My dad wanted me to clean the pool and backwash it before he got home. It's been fun, though."

"Aw, all right, Jim. See you later." Sam looked genuinely disappointed.

As nice as he could be, Jim knew Sam could also be really annoying, and when it came to competition, he was really intense. Still, he would appreciate any nice things from him when he could.

"See ya," both John and Dave said.

Jim watched them ride off and made sure they really went back toward their house before he started down his own driveway. Riding up to the house, he wavered between going back inside and going to see if Charlie was okay. He finally decided he should at least go prepared in case Charlie was in trouble.

He was scared for Charlie.

CHAPTER THIRTEEN
Snakes

GOING THROUGH THE front door, Jim called hello to his mom and then called for Jilly. She was in the kitchen, sitting on the floor and working on some sort of picture collage. She had her legs stuck out like she was doing the splits and was propped up on her left elbow. There was glitter everywhere.

She looked up from her work when Jim entered.

"Hey, Jim. How was it?"

He grimaced and said, "Okay."

Looking at Karen, he saw she was busy cleaning out a drawer, so he gestured for Jilly to follow him. She hopped up surprisingly quickly for the strange position she had been sitting in for who knows how long.

They went up to Jim's room and closed the door quietly.

"You won't believe what I just did with the Whittles," Jim began.

"What?"

"I went looking for the 'thing' they saw in the woods!"

"No!" Her reaction heartened Jim. He was glad to have someone to share his ordeal with and told her the whole story. She giggled when he told her about John thinking it was a bigfoot and Jim trying to convince him otherwise.

"He would be so shocked if he knew about Charlie," she said.

"He can never know." Jim warned.

"I know!" She waved him off with a flick of her hand.

"But, Jilly … I heard Charlie make a roaring sound and so did they."

Her eyes grew wide. "Why did he make that sound? Is he okay? What if he's hurt? Should we go see if he's okay? Let's go!" She was halfway across the room before Jim could stop her.

"Hey! We're going to go, but we need to go prepared. Let's take some first-aid stuff, and we need something to protect ourselves."

"Like what? A gun?"

Jim laughed. "No, we can't take a gun. I was thinking Mom's pepper spray. And maybe a paintball gun."

"A paintball gun? That's not going to do anything."

"Sure it could. Remember when we were trying to get the raccoons to leave the cats alone? The paintball gun scared them off."

"Oh yeah! Okay. Let's go."

"You go get ready. I'll get the stuff."

Jim got a bag and went to the bathroom to find the first-aid supplies. Heading downstairs, Jim looked for where Karen's purse might be. She usually kept it on the bench by the door. Sure enough, it was there. He slipped the pepper spray out, feeling slightly bad about taking her things, but he might need it. Besides, he would only be borrowing it for a little bit. Next, he grabbed his paintball gun from where he had stashed it in the hall closet for easy access in case the raccoons came back.

All set, he went to the kitchen to tell Karen that he would be going to take Jilly to see the print they had found. He was keeping close to the truth.

"Okay, but be quick so that you can take Banjo for a long walk. I took him out earlier, but he seemed to want to go longer," she said.

"Okay, Mom."

He bent down to pet his dog, who was lying in the kitchen looking like he was hoping for some sort of food scrap. His huge cartoon eyes were flitting back and forth between the two people and looking imploringly.

Jilly came bounding down the stairs, but she was hardly making a sound because she was so little. She was dressed in jeans today and a flowery tank top. She had cowboy boots on and was carrying a small purse.

"Let's go," Jim said as he made for the door.

"'Bye, Mom!" Jilly shouted.

They ran outside and down the water well trail. Jim was listening for any sounds in the woods, but heard nothing out of the ordinary. As they walked down the trail, there were birds chirping, squirrels running around and chattering, and rabbits hopping out of the way.

Finally, they came to the turn-off to Charlie's house. Here, they had beaten a small path in the woods that resembled a game trail. Nothing seemed out of place, nothing looked unusual, there were no strange smells.

Jim moved forward carefully, keeping Jilly behind him. She seemed to sense his tension and had ceased the low humming that she had kept up during their walk.

Walking slowly toward Charlie's little home, Jim started calling Charlie's name. They had almost reached his stand of trees and bushes when they heard a shuffling sound to their right. Charlie poked his head around a tree and slowly came around to face them. He was holding his left arm with his right hand and was visibly distraught.

"Charlie! What's wrong?" Jim asked.

Jim and Jilly rushed forward, and Charlie walked forward to meet them. Even beneath all of his thick hair, they could tell that his hand and forearm were very swollen. Jim studied it and then reached tentatively toward his arm. Charlie put out his arm and let Jim inspect it. Jim brushed his hair away in places, looking for some reason for the swelling. Finally, at Charlie's wrist, Jim found two small puncture wounds.

Charlie had been bitten by a snake.

"He was bitten by a snake, Jilly." She gasped and grabbed Charlie's right hand. Jim turned to Charlie. "Charlie, what kind of snake was it?" he asked.

Charlie just looked at Jim with a miserable expression. His face was pinched as he sat down heavily while cradling his arm. Jim knelt down and put a hand on Charlie's shoulder.

"Charlie, what did this to you?" He pointed at his arm. Charlie knew that Jim's inflection meant a question, so he slowly stood again. He turned and walked around to the back of his little home.

Jim and Jilly followed.

Behind his house, Charlie pointed at the ground. There was a dead copperhead snake lying in the grass. Charlie had killed it, but not before it bit him.

Jim knew that this snake was venomous and could do a lot of harm to humans, but he didn't know how it would affect Charlie. Pulling out his first-aid kit, he took out some gauze and some cleaning solution and cleaned the punctures. He took Charlie into his little home and had him lie down. Not sure about how Charlie might react to certain things, he was afraid to give him any pain pills. He brought out a bottle of water and some crackers and gave them to Charlie, who took them appreciatively. He had a small blanket with him and rolled this up to make a pillow for Charlie.

Jilly crouched into the little space and sat down by Charlie's head. She began stroking his hair and humming lightly. Charlie made a murmuring sound and closed his eyes.

They sat with him for an hour, making sure he didn't get any worse. Jim knew that dogs could survive this type of bite and Charlie was much bigger than most people or animals that were bitten. Still, he was worried.

After two hours, Charlie was sleeping, but not very comfortably. When they heard him snoring soundly, they decided they had to get back home. Quietly, they duck-walked out of his little home and began a brisk walk back to the house.

They worried all through dinner and could barely keep up a conversation with their parents. After dinner, it was still light outside, so they decided to go check on him again.

Making it there in record time, they went straight to the entrance of his home. Charlie was still sleeping soundly and didn't seem to be having any other problems.

It bothered Jim that Charlie hadn't stirred when they approached, so he gently shook him awake. Charlie woke with a jerk, opened his eyes partially and grunted, rolled over, and went back to sleep.

When they were heading back to the house, Jim said, "I think he'll be okay. He just needs to sleep it off."

"Oh I hope so. I couldn't bear it if Charlie died."

Jim put an arm around her shoulder and gave her a reassuring squeeze. They made plans to go see him early the next morning.

When the morning came, Jim crept into Jilly's room. This time, Jilly woke up when Jim shook her awake, and they got outside as soon as they could. When they reached Charlie, he was sitting outside of his home against a tree. He waved and smiled, looking much better than the day before.

"Hey! You look better. How are you feeling?"

Jim sat down in front of him and Jilly followed suit. Charlie raised his arm and showed them that the swelling was down. He felt it with his other hand and nodded his head to say that it felt better. Jilly stretched up and hugged Charlie around the neck.

For the rest of the morning, they played little games and tried to have conversations. They walked around and looked at different things. Once, they walked up to find a group of deer eating grass in a clearing and stopped to watch them for several minutes. Silent, the trio was just enjoying where they were and who they were with. The time seemed to be endless, and Jim felt like he could never be happier. Charlie and Jilly were his best friends now, and he loved this time together.

Charlie took them on a path through the woods and showed them things like a spiky tree, which they had never seen before. It was short and thin and covered in brutal-looking thorns. He showed them a place where deer slept and pointed out a hiding rabbit.

They were having a great time until they heard voices.

Deep in the woods and away from the trail, they were able to stay put, hidden from view. They crouched down and hid behind a large tree.

After a few minutes, Jim could make out the voices. The Whittles had trespassed on their land. They were talking quietly but loud enough to be heard.

"I don't care what Jim says anymore. If you guys think you saw a bigfoot, I believe you and I want to find it. It could make us rich." Dave's voice had carried to Jim's ears.

Jim frowned. They were back to believing that it had not been a hunter.

"What if it's not here anymore? What if it moved on?" asked Sam.

"It's here. I bet that's what we heard yesterday," Dave said. "I'm telling you, after all we talked about last night, I'm sure it's a bigfoot. All the signs point to it. John finally told us what he saw, and I believe him. It's probably like some lab experiment that got loose."

"Guys, do we really need to find it?" John was obviously scared. His voice sounded strained and shaky.

So he had broken down and told his brothers.

Jilly looked at Jim horrified. Charlie's eyes had narrowed, and he was sniffing the air. Looking at Jim, he seemed to understand that he was in danger and stayed where he was.

They waited for the Whittles to pass and then began quietly making their way deeper into the woods between their house and the trail. When they felt like they were far enough away, they all crouched between some thick bushes to talk.

"What are they doing here, Jim? They shouldn't be here!" Jilly was outraged.

"They're looking for Charlie. I can't believe it. Those jerks need to stay away!"

Jim was seething. They had no right being on their land and no right to be messing with Charlie.

"What do we do? How do we get rid of them?" Jilly was looking to Jim for ideas.

The whole time they were talking, Charlie was watching them both closely and kept sniffing the air. He would be able to tell if they were coming closer.

"I don't know."

Jim was trying to think of some way to make sure that they stayed away, but he was coming up empty. Finally, he decided what to do.

"You guys stay here. Stay hidden, okay? I'm going to go make them leave."

"Jimmy, be careful."

"I will. It's just the Whittles." He stood up and motioned for them to stay.

"I'll be back, Charlie. You stay with Jilly," he said as he pointed at his little sister.

He stalked angrily through the woods. The Whittles had taken it upon themselves to come onto his land and make trouble for Charlie. He walked in the direction they had gone, and after a few minutes, he thought he heard a twig crunch to his right. Looking, Jim saw nothing, but sensed a presence. Taking a chance, he called out, "Come on out!"

At first, nothing happened. Then all three Whittles edged out from behind trees on either side of the trail. To Jim's complete shock, they all were armed. Dave and Sam had crossbows and John had a recurve bow.

They were hunting Charlie.

"What did you have to blow our cover for?" Of course Dave was in his usual chipper mood, Jim noticed.

"Your cover? For what? You have no business being here, especially with those bows. There's no hunting here."

Sam jumped forward to try to keep the peace.

"Look, Jim. We really think there might be some cool animal over here. Wouldn't it be great if we got it? You guys could be in danger."

"We are in danger. From you guys. Jilly could have been out here and been shot. Get off my land."

"Jim, we don't want any trouble, but we have a lot of hunting experience, and we would appreciate being able to spend some time over here."

Dave was seething behind Sam, but was staying quiet. John was looking like he would rather just leave.

"Sam, no. You can't be here, and especially hunting. I'm sorry, but I'm going to have to tell my parents about this."

"No!" they all yelled in unison.

"Sorry, but you have to leave and you can't come back." He stood there facing them with crossed arms.

Dave came forward with a snarl on his already-unpleasant face.

"Look, you little weasel. We might have stumbled onto something really worth a lot, and you can't stand in our way."

"Dave! Stop." John had finally piped up. "Jim's right. We shouldn't be here like this."

"You shut up too! Jim's been acting all high and mighty for a while now, and I'm sick of it." Rounding on Jim he said, "You're not better than us! If there's some crazy animal running around here, we owe it to everyone to kill it before it kills someone!"

Jim was livid now.

"There's nothing here! You have some crazy ideas based on crappy observations, and you're just trying to play like some big hunter! You have to leave now, or I'm going to call the cops."

Dave took a threatening step forward, and Sam put a hand on his chest. Jim and Dave stood face-to-face for what seemed like minutes and then, finally, Dave stepped back.

"We're leaving. Let's go." They all turned to walk away.

A few steps away, Dave turned and said, "We'll hunt it from our place."

Jim was so mad that he was shaking. He stood for a long time, watching them disappear. When they were gone, he took a deep breath and started walking the trail to his backyard. At a certain place, he turned perpendicular to the path and pushed straight through the woods. He found Jilly and Charlie standing where he had left them. Jilly was holding Charlie's hand and using it to spin like a ballet dancer.

"Jim! Are you okay? What happened?"

Charlie walked forward and searched Jim's face. He seemed to understand that something had upset him.

"Those jerks were hunting Charlie! They had bows and were hiding. They aren't for sure that he's here, well I think John is, but they were here anyway! I told them they were trespassing and had to leave or I would call the cops."

"Oh no! That's so scary!" Jilly was still now and looking very worried. Her little brows were pinched together, and she was wringing her small hands again. "Are you going to tell Mom and Dad?"

"I told them I was, but I'm not sure. I mean, if they asked the Whittles what they were doing, they would tell Mom and Dad that they were hunting a bigfoot."

"Oh. But they don't know he's real! I think you need to tell them. They can help." She was looking up at him with big eyes.

He sighed.

"You're right, Jilly. We'll tell them what the Whittles were doing. Let's get Charlie back."

They were careful as they walked him back to his home. Charlie kept sniffing the air and stopping to listen. They got back, and Charlie turned to look at them.

"Charlie, be careful. You stay hidden and don't let them do anything to you, okay?"

The only thing Charlie understood was Jim's pointing and the concern in his voice. Nodding, Charlie waved and turned to go back into his home.

Jim and Jilly walked back and saw no more signs of the Whittles. During the trip, Jim was thinking about what to do. The first thing he was going to do was tell his parents about the Whittles hunting on their land. That was wrong and dangerous in any situation.

After that, he had no idea.

They reached their house and went in the back door. Banjo bounded over, wagging his long tail, which whacked the peace lily in the pot next to the door over and over.

"Hey, boy. We'll take you for a walk in just a minute," Jim said.

He felt guilty because he usually took Banjo everywhere and always took great care of him. But since he met Charlie, Jim hadn't been spending enough time with him.

"Mom! Where are you?"

They walked into the living room and heard Karen call from her bedroom. She came out carrying her plate of lunch.

"What's going on? Want some lunch?"

"Mom, the Whittles were trespassing on our land. They had bows and were hunting." Jim crossed his arms, and Jilly mimicked him.

"What? They were hunting? That's unacceptable." She started marching to the kitchen. "I'm calling their mom. Tell me exactly what happened."

Jim told her the story and even included the reason they were there.

"So they think there's a bigfoot over here and they've gone crazy. I told them they can't go shooting around here," he explained.

"That's right!" she exclaimed. "Okay, I'm calling."

They followed her outside as she called. She liked to make her calls sitting at the small table out on the front porch, so Jim paced the deck while Jilly visited with the cats. Banjo came outside with them and was sniffing everything in their fenced-in front yard. They listened as she told Tess about what had happened. Apparently, Tess was trying to defend her boys, but Karen was not having it.

"They can't go around hunting on other people's private property! They didn't ask permission and could have killed one of my kids."

Jim was pleased with how this was going with Karen, but he was genuinely shocked that Tess would take her boys' side. They were just plain wrong. He started to see how they got the way they were and that it might be harder than he thought to stop them.

When Karen finally hung up, she was even angrier than when she had started.

"That woman is unbelievable! How she can excuse their behavior is beyond me. We're going to talk to your dad about this when he gets home. We might need to put up a gate and signs, and if they come again, we're calling somebody." She stopped with her hands on her hips and her eyes flashing.

"Wow!" Jilly was shocked. She hadn't seen her mom so angry about something.

"Well really!" She threw up her arms. "Those boys aren't the brightest bulbs, and they could have mistaken one of you for some animal and shot you! I'm not going to have that."

"Go, Mom!" Jim was happy to have her on his side. For a second, he even considered telling her about Charlie and getting her support there, but he quickly realized that the thought of Charlie would scare her, and she might not be so supportive.

They followed Karen into the house, cheering her on, and then helped her with lunch.

Jim felt slightly better about things, but still didn't trust the Whittles.

CHAPTER FOURTEEN
The Ambush

THAT EVENING WHEN Jack came home, they told him everything about the Whittles, and he was so angry that he went to their house to talk with their parents. He returned an hour later.

"I don't think they'll be over here anymore."

He sat down on the couch with a sigh. The family had been sitting in the living room, waiting for news.

"What happened?" Jim asked.

"The parents were trying to make excuses at first, but I told them how it was and that they couldn't come over here to hunt without facing legal problems. The boys agreed not to return and the parents said they would make sure it wouldn't happen again. I don't think we'll be invited to lunch or dinner anytime soon." He laughed lightly.

To their surprise, Karen said, "Oh, what a crying shame," in the most sarcastic tone possible.

After a split second of surprise, they all burst out laughing.

Jim was so glad to have his parents supporting them with this, even though they didn't know the full truth. But it also made him feel guilty.

Lying in bed later, he thought about it. He really wanted them to know the truth, but not yet. It was still too soon and not the right time. But when would the right time be? Charlie seemed to be staying. At least, Jim hoped he was.

They should know soon.

For the next week, nothing surprising happened. Jim was on constant alert for the Whittles, but he never saw them. He and Jilly went to visit Charlie every day, sometimes twice. They were building their fort slowly, and Jack was helping when he could. Charlie seemed fascinated with the whole process. He would help Jim lift the wood and had learned to use the hammer. These were some of the best days of their lives. They were having so much fun with Charlie, and he was really becoming a part of their family.

One day Jim decided it was time to introduce Banjo to Charlie. He put on Banjo's blue harness and took him out on the leash.

"Mom! We're going to the fort! We're taking Banjo!" he called on his way out the door.

"Okay!"

They walked down the water well trail to the tree and called out to Charlie. They had learned that Charlie had excellent hearing and would come within minutes if they called. He seemed always ready to see them.

Today, he slowly approached them and was obviously sniffing Banjo's scent. Banjo smelled Charlie's approach and turned to face him, hackles raised and growling. Jim kept a strong hand on his leash and used the other to slowly pet his head and back.

"It's okay, boy. It's okay. He's a friend. That's Charlie."

Banjo wouldn't take his eyes off Charlie, but Jilly stepped forward and walked toward Charlie. This caused Banjo to try to run forward, but Jim held him back. Barely.

"Banjo, it's okay! See? Charlie's good! We love Charlie!" she said.

Jilly skipped up to Charlie and grabbed his hand to pull him forward. Banjo appeared confused and the growling grew softer. Jilly pulled Charlie in front of Banjo and stood there stroking his arm.

"See? He's good."

Charlie was wary of Banjo, having encountered the neighbor's dogs weeks before, but he looked at Jim and Jilly and seemed to trust them. Banjo slowly stopped growling and looked up at Jim as if to ask him what was going on.

Jim petted him gently and said, "Good, boy! We're all going to get along."

Jilly stepped up to Banjo and pet him and then went back to pet Charlie. Banjo was a smart dog. He sat down and his hair settled.

Charlie stayed where he was and looked at Banjo.

"Charlie, this is Banjo. He's our dog and we love him." Jim was trying to introduce them properly. "We pet him like this. See?" He was stroking Banjo's head and playing with his ears.

Jilly pulled Charlie a little closer. He seemed a bit reluctant, but was allowing her to guide him. Jilly had one hand on Banjo while the other held Charlie's hand. She pulled him closer still, and then he was within reach of Banjo.

Jim made sure to have a tight grip on Banjo.

Finally, Banjo leaned forward and began sniffing close to Charlie, who slowly put a hand out. They stayed like that for a minute before Charlie reached out and petted Banjo's head. Banjo's muscles tightened, but slowly relaxed.

After a minute, Charlie pulled away.

Charlie and Banjo looked at Jim as if to say, "We did it!" Jim smiled at both of them and nodded at Charlie. He patted Banjo twice on the head and told him he was a good boy.

Introductions over, Jim took Banjo to the tree and secured his leash to it. Jim and Jilly began working on the tree fort and trying to communicate to Charlie through hand gestures. Charlie surprised them by taking a piece of wood and holding it in place for Jim. Stunned, Jim said, "Thanks, Charlie."

"Charlie! Let me try something," Jilly said. She explained that she finally had had enough and sat Charlie down to brush his hair. Jim watched Charlie as he sat there getting his hair pulled by her aggressive brushing, but, to his credit, he never uttered a sound. He let Jilly rake through his hair and jabber away at him far longer than Jim expected. When she was done, she pulled a mirror to show Charlie her work, and he pretended to look happy with it. Maybe he really was.

Banjo was becoming more comfortable with Charlie and had allowed him to pet him again. Jim really wanted them to get along. It was a testament to how much each of them trusted Jim that they both were giving each other a chance.

When it was time for lunch, Karen brought them sandwiches and chips with chocolate milk and chocolate chip cookies. Charlie hid while their mom visited. When she left, he came back out.

As hungry as Jim was, he split his food with Charlie. Jilly gave him half of hers too. They laughed while he tried each item. He enjoyed the peanut butter sandwich, and they giggled while he worked the sticky stuff in his mouth. They found that the chocolate milk was his particular favorite. He made happy hooting noises as he drank, and he seemed to relish the cookie. Jim realized he probably had never had chocolate in his life.

"What do you eat, Charlie?" he asked. "We don't really know what you eat other than those berries and some leaves. That can't be enough."

Jim hadn't really thought about it until now. He just knew that Charlie had always been capable of finding food and never seemed to be hungry. This was all very new to him, but he felt stupid for not thinking about it earlier.

Of course, Charlie didn't answer. He kept taking small bites of his cookie, savoring each bite. Jilly clapped her hands in delight at his enjoyment.

Jim was thinking about Charlie, but his reverie was cut short by Jack's voice.

"Hey, guys! Are you still there?"

Charlie jumped up and waved goodbye as he darted into the woods. As he passed Banjo, he gave him one final pet, and Banjo actually wagged his tail.

"We're here! You're home early!"

Jim was sad to see Charlie go, but happy to have Jack home early. They were able to work for a good while and got a lot done. The fort was taking shape now that the floors were finished and much of the frame was up. They thought they could have it done in a couple of days.

"You really got a lot done without me. How did you manage that?" Jack asked.

Jim realized that Charlie had helped out a lot and it might look suspicious that he had gotten that much hard work done without Jack. Charlie had been able to do a lot of the heavy lifting and any of the high reaching.

"I did? Cool. I wanted to do my part so you wouldn't have to work so hard." He hoped Jack didn't go too far into it.

He didn't. "This is going to be a great fort! We should make it cozy inside, too. Right, Jilly?" Jack said.

"Yeah! I'll make it pretty!"

Jim groaned. "It's not supposed to be pretty, Jilly."

"Shhh!"

She skipped along in front of them as they went back to the house. Banjo ran forward to match her pace, and Jim was pulled behind.

Later, Jim enjoyed a delicious steak dinner with his family and wondered if Charlie would eat steak. They had brownies a la mode outside on their deck. The fireflies were dancing and crickets were singing loudly. They could hear the tree frogs and bull frogs croaking. It was a fantastic evening.

Until yells filled the air.

The terrifying sounds echoed eerily from across the lake. There was a sudden crashing noise as something huge splashed into the water, and the yells intensified and drew closer.

"What in the world?" Jack was standing up. The family all got up from their comfortable chairs around the deck table and went to the railing.

"Get it! It's in the water!" They could barely make out what Dave was yelling.

There was an unmistakable sound of something big sloshing through water and then it sounded like it had reached the other side and was pulling its wet bulk from the water. Now the sound of something rushing through bushes in their backyard.

Jim's spine tingled as he realized that they were most probably chasing Charlie. His mind was reeling at why Charlie might have crossed the lake in the first place.

Along with all of the ruckus was a strange thwunking sound. Jim suddenly realized it was arrows cutting through the air and hitting trees and the ground. They were shooting at Charlie!

A spotlight was shining wildly in their backyard and seemed to be coming closer. The Whittles were crossing the lake in their boat.

Without thinking, Jim shouted, "Charlie!" He took off around the railing and down the steps into the dark backyard.

"Jim! Come back! It's dangerous!" Karen was screaming at him.

Jim kept yelling Charlie's name and was running to the tree line to the left. He could hear the rushing sounds in the woods halt and then change course. Charlie was coming to Jim.

"Charlie! Come here!"

"Who's Charlie?" Jack was suddenly by his side. Looking around, he saw Karen and Jilly had joined him too.

"Mom, Dad, don't freak out. Charlie's our friend and we need to save him from these lunatics!"

"Is he a dog? What's going on?" Jack was straining his eyes to see what Jim was talking about.

They could hear the paddles of the boat thunk on the pier, and Jim knew they were jumping out to chase Charlie.

Jim looked at Jilly, whose eyes were huge and reflecting the moonlight. She seemed at a loss for words and then she said, "He saved me and Jim."

Jack's eyes narrowed. "What is he?"

"Dad, they're coming! Stop them while I hide Charlie. Please, you have to trust me!"

He didn't wait for a reply; he just ran straight into the woods to where he thought Charlie was. Charlie materialized in front of him with wide eyes. He had probably never been hunted before.

Jim grabbed his hand and pulled him through the woods. They went around the fence at the front of the house and over the driveway. Jim led him over to the door of the garage and pushed him through it.

Charlie had never been inside before, Jim guessed. He looked all around himself with wonder.

"Stay here! You need to stay here." He kept pointing at the ground and Charlie, hoping that he would understand. Turning, he then flew out the door, slamming it, and down the driveway to the house. He went through the house and out the back door to check on his family.

"Dad! What's going on?"

He could see them standing a few feet from the deck. They turned and started hurrying back up the steps.

"Those are the worst kids I've ever come across!" Jack was stomping up the steps and began to cross the deck. "I'm calling their idiot dad right now."

"How dare they talk to you that way," Karen cut in.

"What happened?" Jim was getting impatient.

"Your dad called out to them to stop and leave right away. Then they came up and told us they saw some bigfoot thing and were going to go kill it and that we couldn't stop them." Karen was practically shaking with anger.

Jack snorted. "Bigfoot. They're idiots! So then they're standing there with their bows and telling me I have to step aside while they hunt."

"I bet it was Dave doing all the talking," Jim said.

"Nope. The other two punks were chiming in too. So I got really mad and yelled at them to leave now while I call the sheriff and their parents."

"They finally turned around and went back to their boat, but not without some name-calling," Karen finished.

Jim was shocked that they had actually been so disrespectful. He knew they weren't that bright and could be mean, especially Dave, but Sam and John were followers more than anything. For the boys to go to these extremes meant they must have seen Charlie clearly and knew what they were up against.

They were throwing all caution to the wind to get Charlie.

In the house, they were all still standing because they were too upset and excited to sit. Jack finally spun to Jim.

"What is this all about? Who's Charlie?"

Jim looked at Jilly. This was it. They had to tell them about Charlie.

"Okay. Remember the day that I fell out of the tree and got stuck?" His parents were now standing in front of him, watching him closely.

"Yes." They looked at each other.

"Well, I was out there to look for something that I thought might be out there. I was looking for a bear because of what Jilly and Mom had seen … and some other things."

"YOU HAVE A BEAR?" both of his parents roared at this thought.

"No! No! It's not a bear. I went out there, thinking there was some animal out there that would reasonably explain what Jilly saw. I fell and would have been stuck there for a long time if Charlie hadn't come and saved me. Charlie's … Charlie's a bigfoot. He pulled me down and saved me."

It was out. He had told them.

They were staring at him like he had just sprouted a second head. Jim was holding his breath. The minutes seemed to tick by until Karen made a sputtering sound and Jack laughed a loud, dry laugh. He sounded nervous.

"A bigfoot? You're kidding me."

"I'm not kidding you, Dad. He's real. He's a bigfoot, and he's nice and our friend."

"Daddy, Mommy, he saved me from a mommy pig that tried to kill me," Jilly piped up. "He lets me do his hair sometimes." They were now looking at Jilly as if she was a purple alien.

"Where is he? Can we see him?" Jack asked.

Jim got the idea that they thought their kids had lost their minds. They were asking for proof that they didn't think existed.

"Yeah, Dad. He's in the garage."

"In the garage?" Jack's eyes were wild, and he looked close to panic. "You're sounding like those crazy Whittle boys."

"They're crazy all right, but not about this—this is real."

Jim was suddenly feeling oddly confident and strong. He knew he should be scared and upset, but this was real, and he knew Charlie would never hurt them. His parents were rational people who would eventually see this.

"Let's go meet him." Jim started to lead the way.

"I'm bringing my gun."

"No, Dad! You can't. He's good and would never hurt any of us."

"I'm not going unarmed to meet a bigfoot."

"You have to or I won't let you."

At this, Jack looked incredulously at him. After a few seconds, Jack calmed down. Something in Jim's eyes was calming him and letting him know that it would be okay. Jim seemed to be in control of the situation and this was giving them strength. They both nodded.

Jim said, "Let's go," and walked them out the front door. They all walked in silence down the driveway and around the Y to the other side leading to the garage.

When they reached the door, Jim paused.

"He's very big, very smart, and very nice. Don't be alarmed and just be calm and nice."

His parents just looked at him with wide eyes. They were sticking close to each other and Jim. He noticed they had Jilly behind them, but she was trying to work herself in front.

Jim took a breath and opened the door.

Charlie was sitting cross-legged on the cool floor of the garage in a clear space. He stayed seated as they entered, like he somehow sensed that by sitting he would look less threatening.

Jim entered, and his parents stayed behind him. He heard a sharp intake of breath from both of them and then Karen made a small, stifled screaming sound. Charlie stayed still.

"Hi, Charlie. These are my parents." Jim turned to his parents, "Mom, Dad, this is Charlie."

Jilly skipped forward.

"Hi, Charlie!" She was positively beaming. Charlie beamed back at her and waved, but remained seated.

"Jim, this thing's huge," Jack breathed behind him.

"Dad, he's not a thing. He's Charlie. Say hi to him."

Jack looked scared, but cleared his throat and said, "Hi, Charlie."

Charlie seemed to sense the tension and the fear from Jim's parents. He screwed up his face in concentration and seemed to be working on getting some sound out. Finally, he said very clearly, "Jiiimm." Karen gasped, and Jack's mouth dropped open.

Jilly squealed with delight and ran forward to hug Charlie around the neck. As she did so, Karen shot forward, but when she saw Jilly and Charlie together, she stopped. His parents now wore identical looks of awe. Jilly pulled away and turned back to her parents.

Charlie unfolded his long legs and began to stand. When he reached his full height, Jim's parents gasped again at his impressive size. Charlie looked very shy in this moment with the two adults studying him. He was holding his hands together and almost wringing them. His eyes were flitting between Jim's parents and the ground.

Finally, Karen spoke.

"He looks sort of young in the face," she said.

"Yeah, I think he's pretty young for one of them. He had parents who died and two siblings, but they were chased out of their home by fire and were split up somehow. We don't know how yet," Jim said.

Karen and Jack looked at their son in surprise.

"He can talk?" asked Jack.

"No, he's kinda learning, but we communicate pretty well through drawing."

"Amazing," Jack said.

They were taking it pretty well.

Jack finally moved forward and stood beside Jilly, who was looking at Charlie with complete adoration.

"Hello, my name is Jack." He pointed to himself as he said it, and Charlie seemed to understand. Charlie pointed back at him as Jack said, "Jack," again. He turned to his wife and pointed at her, saying, "Karen."

Karen stepped forward and put her hands on Jilly's shoulders while she stared up at Charlie's face. "He has such a kind face. He saved both of you?"

"Yeah. He saved me from the tree, and Jilly from the biggest pig I've ever seen. She really was in trouble."

Karen spoke to Charlie.

"Thank you—for saving my children."

Charlie just looked down at her face with a slight smile. He probably had no idea what she was saying, but he seemed to like her tone of voice.

"What are we going to do with him? Where does he live?" Jack was always practical.

"He's been living in the woods, far back, almost to the Black's fence. He has a little bed area in the middle of some bushes and trees. After what the Whittles have been doing, I don't think he's safe there."

"I have to agree," Jack said.

"Dad, can he sleep in here tonight?" Jim was hoping that he would be able to lie safely in there and avoid any trouble with the Whittles.

"Does he eat vegetables? Where did he get those?" Karen was pointing at a small pile of carrots and tomatoes that were behind Charlie. Jim hadn't noticed them before, but Charlie must have had them in one of his hands as he was rushing through the woods to escape the Whittles.

"I don't know. Where did you get these?" Jim asked Charlie. Charlie just pointed toward the lake.

Karen offered up an explanation.

"The Foresters have a vegetable garden. He must have taken some from there."

"That's why you kept going across the lake! You were getting food! I had no idea or I would have brought you some. That's why you're in trouble now." Jim felt horrible. He groaned.

"You couldn't have known." Karen said consolingly.

"He had been seen a couple of times by the Whittles, but they weren't sure. I didn't know he was still going over there—and for food." Jim's shoulders drooped in guilt.

"It's okay, Jim." Jack put a comforting hand on his shoulder. "This is incredible. I wonder how many more like him are out there." Jack was just like Jim had been—curious.

Jilly had started walking around the garage, collecting old blankets and camping supplies to make a bed for Charlie. She laid them out, made a nest for him, and told him to lie there. She ended up lying down and curling up to feign sleep in order to show him what to do, which brought a laugh from the group.

Charlie sat down on his bed and looked up at everybody.

Karen turned to leave. "I'm going to get him some food. He obviously likes fruit and vegetables."

Jim was surprised at how quickly she had taken to caring for Charlie. She was such a mom.

Jack began to slowly sit down in front of Charlie. He was just staring, taking him in.

This was what Jim loved about his parents. They were, by many standards, nuts. Jack and Karen had very open minds, and they definitely would need them for this. They loved adventure and anything unique. Charlie was definitely unique.

"Where did he live before this? Where is he from?" Jack looked to Jim for answers.

"I'm not sure, but I know there were some wildfires out west. I assume one of those areas. Maybe here? Maybe Arizona?"

"I wonder how we can find out. You say he was separated from his siblings? Brothers, sisters?"

"Yeah. I don't know which, exactly. I think one of each."

"I bet he misses them."

"I would."

They sat for a while, watching Jilly move around Charlie trying to make him more comfortable until Karen entered with a large Tupperware container of fruits and vegetables. She had included some granola bars as well.

Charlie's eyes grew wide at the feast. He gently accepted the container and began poking at the different items with his large finger to see what was there. He looked up at Karen with a smile. Hungrily, he chomped into a large piece of melon and smacked his lips with joy.

Jim felt whole now. His entire family knew about Charlie and wanted to help. He was no longer hiding anything. Now if only they could take care of the Whittles.

They spent several minutes trying to teach Charlie how to open the door in case he needed to go outside. He caught on quickly. Jack was becoming more comfortable with Charlie already. Once, without thinking, he reached out, grabbed Charlie's hand and guided it to the lock, and then quickly pulled back. He then went ahead and slowly put his hand on Charlie's. Grinning at Jim, he somehow looked years younger.

When they felt Charlie was settled, they said goodnight and left him in his new room.

"Is this really happening?" Karen asked. She was grinning like Jack and seemed exhilarated.

"It's incredible, isn't it?" Jim replied.

He looked at his parents.

"I'm really sorry I've been keeping this from you. I thought you might think I was crazy at first and then I was scared of what you would think of him. I was wrong."

They were quiet for a moment.

Finally, Jack said, "I understand why you did what you did, but know that you can always tell us anything."

Jim felt like a huge weight had been lifted off his shoulders. He suddenly felt very sleepy and told everyone goodnight.

They all went to bed happy and tired.

CHAPTER FIFTEEN
Friends and Foe

THE NEXT MORNING, Jim went downstairs and found his parents talking at the kitchen table. They were discussing what Charlie might be.

"He could be the missing link or something like that," Karen was saying.

Jack continued her thought. "Is he even human? Is he like an ape thing? Scientists would love to get a hold of him. He's the most amazing find in recent history!"

"We can't do that to Charlie!" Jim cut in. He couldn't help himself. There was no way he was going to make Charlie some science experiment.

"No, no. We wouldn't do that. I'm just saying he's that important. I kind of think there's a reason they've been hidden for so long, and since they've been so good at it, they deserve their anonymity," Jack explained.

"Okay. Good." Jim sat down beside them. "Have you seen him today?"

"No. We thought we should wait for you since he knows you best."

"Okay. We should take him food and water. Can … can I bring him over here?"

His parents looked at each other as if this thought had never crossed their minds.

"I don't know. How will he react, do you think? What about Banjo?" Jack asked.

"They've met. I introduced them, and they get along. He's really good, and I think he adapts pretty well. He could just come in to eat."

"Let's see how he did in the garage first. He may not like being inside very much." Karen was still being cautious.

"Okay. I'm going to check on him."

Jack stood. "We'll go with you."

First, they gathered up some water and breakfast foods that Charlie might like. They had fruits and vegetables and had included some cereals to try. These were all placed nicely on a tray with napkins. Karen was big on using napkins.

They walked across to the garage and knocked on the door. The door was now unlocked, and Charlie was sitting inside on his bed. He had brought a foam pool float over and had added it to his bedding for more comfort. He had gathered old toys and books around himself and was currently examining an old book about a puppy. It had bright pictures that seemed to be captivating him.

"Morning, Charlie!" Jim walked over and sat down with him. He pulled the book over so that he could see it. "I liked this one too."

His parents said hello and walked over. Karen bent down and presented the tray of foods to Charlie, whose eyes widened. He looked at Jim as if he couldn't believe that was all for him. Reaching out, he grabbed a banana and tried to give it to Jim first, who declined, then Jim's parents.

"No, no. That's yours! It's for you." Jack was smiling.

Charlie sniffed it. He broke the banana in half and then realized it needed peeling, so he started peeling it. He crammed it into his mouth and made a satisfied grunting sound. They watched him for a little while as he tried the different cereals and ate everything off his tray.

Jim noticed that he had organized things in little piles. He had some Legos and other little pieces of toys in one pile, cars and small play-sets, like Jim's old airport, in another pile, and books in a third pile.

"He organized everything," said Jack.

"Yeah. I saw." Jim said. They shared a glance. Charlie was more amazing every day.

Charlie stretched his arms and got up. He handed the tray to Karen with a small bow that seemed to indicate respect and appreciation. He walked past them to the door and pointed.

Jim jumped up and went to the door.

"He wants to go outside. I wonder why."

"Maybe bathroom break?" Jack suggested.

"Maybe he likes being outside," Karen added.

Jim opened the door, and Charlie walked outside. He turned and looked at Jim and his parents, waved, and turned to walk across the driveway toward the woods.

"Charlie! Where are you going? Are you coming back?" Jim was worried and wondering why he wasn't staying.

Charlie turned and waved again, then disappeared into the woods, leaving the Thomas family feeling disappointed and confused.

When Jilly woke up, she was upset to hear that Charlie had gone and that she had missed their last visit. She spent the morning pouting and drawing pictures. Jim noticed they were all of Charlie.

Jim spent the morning telling his parents of every meeting he had had with Charlie. They sat quietly, listening intently. They heard every detail of his visits and of Jilly's encounter with the pig. Karen gasped when she heard the danger that Jilly had been in, but she teared up when Jim told her how Charlie had saved her.

"My baby could have died!" She put an arm around Jilly.

Jim then told them about the snake bite and how Charlie had survived something that could kill a human. What really struck Jim was how quickly he had recovered.

Jack offered some ideas. "They don't always kill dogs. He might have thicker skin or some sort of tolerance. He's huge, too. That's interesting."

By lunchtime, there was still no Charlie. They all seemed to be waiting for his return, although he never indicated that he would return. Jim kept thinking about Charlie's life before this. He was a bigfoot, something that most people didn't believe in, and he had a small family. Who knew how many others there were, but there couldn't be many. Charlie had spent his life away from humans and now found himself without a family and having to survive on his own. He had found the Thomas family, but it wasn't his own. He had to miss his siblings.

After lunch, the family went outside to swim. It was a hot summer Saturday and swimming seemed to be the only logical thing to do. They had a relaxing time, but Jim knew there were moments where each of them felt a little anxious as they wondered about Charlie.

A sudden barking sound came from the woods across the backyard, and the neighbor's three dogs came streaking across the yard toward their home with their tails tucked. Charlie came bounding out behind them and stopped when he saw the family. Waving, he strode over.

He stayed a little ways away and looked a little unsure about the whole swimming pool idea. Jim climbed out of the pool and walked over to Charlie. He pulled him over to the pool deck and had him stand at the edge of the pool. Dipping his toes in the pool,

Jim motioned for Charlie to do the same, which he did. Charlie then bent down and sniffed the pool water. He made a chuffing sound, and Jim realized that the chlorine might be bothering him.

Jim jumped back in the pool. Jilly was sitting on the steps of the pool and tried to get Charlie to at least sit with her, but he seemed hesitant. He watched them play in the water for a short time. Finally the heat got to him, so he put his legs in the water. He started splashing his hands in the cool, clean water and smiled.

After a while of that, he finally plunged himself in the water up to his shoulders. Jim and Jilly were thrilled, and their parents were laughing. They spent a good while playing with Charlie in the water. They all noticed that he had been pretty dirty, but the soak was cleaning him. He was quite a good swimmer.

Charlie stayed around the house for the rest of the day and even went to the garage for a nap. Jim realized that he was quickly becoming used to living with the family.

They decided to have dinner on the back deck and brought Charlie around to join them. He sat in one of the chairs, but barely fit.

To Jim, it was a magical night. He was thrilled to have his family together with Charlie. Jilly and his parents went inside to clean up, leaving Charlie and Jim outside to enjoy the evening air. They were listening to the crickets sing and were leaning back to look at the stars.

Jim was totally relaxed and content.

He suddenly remembered that they had brownies for dessert and went in to grab one for himself and one for Charlie. He was going to give Charlie ice cream on top of his and couldn't wait to see what he thought of the cold treat.

He scooped a couple of heaping spoonfuls of vanilla ice cream on each brownie and was carrying them to the door when he heard Charlie roar.

Everyone froze and then, all at once, they were scrambling for the door to get outside. Jim was first to the door after dropping the brownies and once outside, he saw Charlie leaping over the railing with a thud and running to the woods. He could hear multiple bodies moving quickly through the woods ahead of Charlie. They seemed to be moving in the general direction of the lake, but he couldn't see anything.

"Charlie!" Jim yelled.

He looked around for any signs of what made Charlie roar and saw an arrow stuck in the wooden railing in front of where Charlie had been sitting. If it had been two inches higher, it would have struck Charlie in the head.

It was the Whittles.

They had come and intruded upon their perfect evening and were obviously intent on not only trapping or proving Charlie existed, but killing him. This angered Jim beyond anything he had ever felt before, and it obviously had angered Charlie enough that he was actively pursuing them.

What a nightmare.

"Charlie! Charlie!" Jilly was screaming.

She was dancing in place and looked absolutely panicked. Jim's parents were looking scared and pale as well. It was unnerving hearing multiple people moving invisibly through the woods as they hunted Charlie.

Jim didn't think; he just started running down the steps of the deck and out into the yard. Karen's screams pierced through the blind rage he was feeling enough that he slowed and could hear Jack yelling at him to slow down.

Turning back, he saw Jack was following. He had picked up the spotlight that had been on the table beside them and was shining it into the woods.

They couldn't see anything, but they could now hear yelling. The words were muffled, but it sounded like someone was trying to attract attention and someone else was yelling orders. The struggling group seemed to be moving down the bank of the lake, and Jim couldn't seem to gain on them.

It was agony, but he kept running.

Suddenly, a huge roar erupted that made Jim's spine tingle and every hair stand up on his body. There was some thudding, some crashing in the woods, and the thunk of what sounded like something wooden hitting a boat.

Charlie roared again, and Jim could hear Jilly scream behind him.

Jim and Jack started making their way through the woods as quickly as they could while still being careful not to get shot. They could hear an intense struggle, and Charlie was still roaring. He sounded absolutely terrifying. Jim couldn't see how the Whittles weren't scared out of their minds. They began to see lights shining, and Jim knew they were getting close.

Jim shouted out, "Stop! Leave him alone!" It didn't help, not that he expected it to.

"This is Jack Thomas! DO NOT SHOOT! Leave him alone!"

Even Jack's authority had no effect. The struggle was continuing on, and it seemed like Jim was moving in slow motion.

Charlie roared again, and the Whittles let out an excited yelp. They heard what sounded like a soft whooshing sound and then Charlie's yells grew fainter. There was a thudding sound, along with some splashing, like something big landed hard on a boat in the water. Then came the sound of oars splashing. What could they possibly be doing?

Finally, the lights were getting brighter, and Jim broke through the tree line. It took him a moment to figure out what he was seeing.

In the middle of the lake, the Whittles had Charlie tied up and lying in the bottom of their boat.

"Hey! Bring him back! You can't do this!" Jim was panicked.

The Whittles reached the edge of the lake, and the three of them worked hard to roll Charlie out of the boat. They had an ATV waiting on shore. It had a small trailer hitched to it and the ramp was down. They were now working to roll Charlie up the ramp and into the trailer. They had been planning this.

Jim turned around and started running back the way they had come. Jack caught up and they were running side by side.

He turned to Jim and said, "We need to get to the car. You get the keys; I'll meet you there."

They crashed into their backyard and didn't slow down. Passing Jilly and Karen, Jim screamed, "Get to the Jeep! They've got Charlie!" He saw them start to run around the house while he went inside to get the keys from the kitchen drawer.

Inside the house, Banjo followed Jim around frantically. The dog knew something bad was happening, but Jim couldn't stop. Jack had followed him in and passed him to go to his bedroom. Jim's lungs were on fire, but he kept moving as fast as he could. He fumbled for a minute during his search, but then grabbed the keys as Jack came back through the bedroom door.

They both ran through the front door and out the front gate. When they got to the car, the girls were waiting for them, and they all got in. Jack turned on the car and gunned the engine as he backed very quickly down the drive.

"What happened? Where's Charlie?" Karen was scared and breathing hard. Jilly's face was pink, and she had tears streaming down her cheeks. Jim could hear her gulping breaths as she cried quietly.

"They've got Charlie," Jim answered. "They trapped him and tied him up. I think they tranquilized him or something. At least I hope that's all it was because he got quiet and stopped fighting. They were putting him on a trailer to take him somewhere."

Jack sped down the road and turned left down the Whittle's street. He took all the twists along the way much faster than was really safe, but they were lucky they didn't hit anything. They made it to the Whittle's house in a couple of minutes and went straight down the driveway.

Jack skidded to a stop and jumped out of the car. The rest of them followed immediately behind him as he went around the house and into the backyard. The ATV was nowhere to be seen. There was nothing but silence all around them.

Jim had no idea where they could have taken Charlie.

Jack went back around the house to the front door and banged on it. There was a shuffling sound inside and then the door opened and Paul and Tess Whittle were standing there in their night clothes, looking very confused.

"Where are your boys? They took something of ours."

"Jack? What do you mean? Took what?" Paul was blinking rapidly and seemed to have no idea what Jack was talking about. Jim thought he looked like a pasty lizard with his dark, blinking eyes and thin mouth set tight.

"They took … a pet of ours. They came over and took it from our yard, onto their boat, and then took it away on an ATV. Where could they have gone?"

Tess finally found her voice.

"I have no idea. Why would they have done something like that? That doesn't sound like my boys. They usually play in the woods, but I don't know where."

"We're going to take a look back there." Jack started to walk back around the house, but Paul stopped him.

"You can't go back there! This is private property, and you all seem pretty upset, but I'm sure this is just a misunderstanding."

"We're going to look for where they took him. You need to stay out of our way."

"Look, Jack. I'll talk to my boys and find out what happened, but I can't let you back there. I don't want to, but I'll call the police if you don't get back in your car and drive away from here."

Jack turned stony and stared at Paul for several seconds. Finally, he said, "Okay, Paul, but we're not done here." Turning around, he led the family back to the car.

CHAPTER SIXTEEN
The Search

"DAD! WE CAN'T leave! They have Charlie!" Jim was feeling beaten and scared.

"I know! We have to leave this area right now, but we're coming back. We just have to be careful about it."

Jack backed out and took off back to their house. When they got home, they poured out of the car and stood there looking dazed.

"We can go by boat," Jack said. "We have to look for where they're keeping him."

"Let's go now!" Jim was dying inside. He felt like whatever they did, it would be too late to keep Charlie from either becoming a zoo exhibit or a trophy.

"We need to be smart about this." Karen was still breathing hard and trying to calm Jilly. "Those boys are so crazy right now. Would they hurt us to keep him?"

She had a point, Jim thought. They had no problem shooting at the house and seemed to have a blatant disregard for the rights of Charlie and his parents' authority.

Jim finally had to say, "Maybe."

"This is insane!" Jack yelled. He started pacing in the driveway. He ran his hands through his hair and stopped. "We need to move quickly. They could be getting ready to call someone to take Charlie. They could be planning to kill him, who knows? I knew those little punks were no good. Their parents are morons!"

Jim was shocked. He hadn't heard him speak badly about them yet. Jack was always pretty laid-back and easygoing.

Suddenly, Jim had a plan. At least the start of a plan.

"Let's go carefully across the lake in the boat. We can take flashlights, but only use them when we really need them. I think you should be armed, Dad."

"I already am. Got my gun when we went back in the house."

Nobody spoke as they thought through the plan. It was the best shot they had. It's not like they could call the police and say that the Whittles stole their bigfoot.

As they thought, Jim was acutely aware of the crickets that usually sounded so soothing, but now seemed to be screeching so loudly that they were hurting his ears. He kept thinking the noise would make it easier to sneak around the woods without detection, but harder for them to hear anything that might indicate where the Whittles were. It was a double-edged sword.

At last, Jack spoke. "Let's go, but just Jim and me. You two stay here in case Charlie gets away and comes back for help."

They all sprinted for the house, where Jim and Jack gathered flashlights. Jack checked his pistol again. He would never use it unless his life or his family's lives were in danger, but with things as uncertain as they were, everyone was glad he was armed. They also had their phones so that they could call for help should they need it. Karen was on call in case they needed the Jeep on short notice.

As they turned to walk out the door, Jim turned to Jilly, who was huddled on the couch in tears.

"Jilly, we'll get him. No matter how long it takes, we'll get him back and he'll be okay."

She finally sat up and looked into Jim's eyes.

"Please, please, Jimmy, get him back. He's my best friend besides you."

"I'll try my best."

She lay back down and curled up again, so Jim turned and left. He knew how she felt and quietly hoped that he could come through for his little sister.

He and Jack walked out the back door and down the deck steps. They crossed the yard with determined strides and quietly got into their boat.

Keeping the splashing to a minimum, they paddled to the right, around the edge of the lake, and crossed in the darkest spot they could find in order to stay hidden. It was hard because the full moon lit up the entire lake and much of the woods.

Jim hopped silently out of the boat. Grabbing the rope, he pulled the boat ashore so that Jack could hop out. They pulled it away from the bank and hid it in a clump of bushes.

Jack nodded, and Jim began running along the bank until he got past the fence that delineated the Whittle's property from the land directly across from the Thomas family.

As soon as they could, they slipped into the cover of the woods.

They decided to move along the neighbor's fence toward the road that ran somewhat parallel to the lake. Moving stealthily, they strained their ears to hear any sign of the boys and Charlie.

After twenty minutes of walking, they had found no sign of them.

They moved along the woods near the road, hoping for something, but Jim knew the Whittles would be deeper in the woods. As they walked, they went diagonally across the woods, back toward the lake. Still nothing. An hour went by, and they were approaching the Whittle's home. They could see the lights were on in the house and the cars were out front.

Nobody had left and nobody had come.

They walked along the tree line back down to the lake and saw nothing. A sudden barking scared Jim out of his skin. The Whittle's two big dogs charged at them. The wind had shifted and was blowing enough to take their scent to the house.

Jim and Jack began running back to their boat. The dogs cut them off at the bank of the lake and began barking madly until Jim finally got them settled. They now were quiet, but stayed with them annoyingly all the way back to the boat. The dogs were weird and skittish. Any movement made them flinch and their body language threatened that they would begin barking again.

Jim and Jack retreated back to their side of the lake and re-grouped. They went back to the house to talk things over and come up with a new plan of attack.

When they entered the house, Banjo jumped up to greet them. He had been waiting by the door and watching with his huge eyes. He knew something bad was happening.

Jilly and Karen were next. They ran up hoping to see Charlie or hear good news, but Jack shook his head.

"Where is he?" Jilly practically screamed. Her voice was high and squeaky.

"We don't know yet. We're going to go back and check the other side of their property. We got ambushed by the dogs and had to get out of there before they got too loud."

"Jack, this is crazy." Karen was understandably very con-cerned about her husband and son trying to rescue Charlie.

"I know, Karen, but it's just wrong what they did. We have to get Charlie back."

"I know, but it's still crazy."

They looked at each other for several seconds, then each nodded.

"Mom, Charlie's special, and we have to save him." Jilly was staring up at her mother.

"I know." She grabbed Jilly and put her arms around her shoulders.

Jack grabbed two cups and filled them with ice water. He gave one to Jim who accepted it gratefully.

"Let's look around on the other side of the house," Jack said. "They most likely would stay on their own property—that would be the safest and give them the most privacy."

Jim had to agree. That was the most logical place to look next, but he didn't remember seeing any structures that could hold Charlie or hearing the Whittles say anything about one.

They grabbed their flashlights again and headed back out.

As Jim walked across the yard, he remembered when he had first heard Charlie's whooping sound. That seemed so long ago. That was back when he thought that Charlie was actually a bear. Jim snuffed out a quiet laugh despite the circumstances.

They reached the boat and decided to lift it and carry it down their back trail to a spot on the other side of the Whittle's home. There, they could enter the water out of sight of the Whittle's open backyard and pier. The boat was heavier than Jim thought it would be. They had to stop and rest along the way, but finally they made it to a spot where they felt safe to enter the water.

Being as quiet as possible, they set the boat on the bank and pushed it into the water. Jim entered first and Jack pushed the boat all the way into the water and hopped spryly into the back. Paddling as quietly as possible, they darted straight across the lake and into a small cove that had a lot of tree cover. Here, they tied the boat off and climbed up a small incline to the woods above.

Looking around, they saw nothing, heard nothing.

They began walking straight down the tree line and then they walked diagonally across again. And again, they came up with nothing. To ensure that they covered all the ground, they walked down to the road and followed it a ways in a zigzag pattern. Another hour had passed with still no sign of the boys or Charlie.

Feeling like they were missing something, they went back for another pass. After twenty minutes, they found a spot and sat down. They were tired, but wired and were hoping for anything at the moment. Listening hard, they tried to will some sort of sign to appear.

After half an hour, they felt they had to give up this area.

Jack had another idea.

"Let's go stake out the house again. See what's happening now."

"Okay."

Jim was dejected. This was a horrible nightmare, and he wanted to wake up. He followed Jack, still straining with all of his senses for some sort of sign of Charlie.

As they reached the house, they found a large tree that would conceal them nicely and settled behind it. After five minutes of waiting, they were shocked to see Dave pass by the kitchen window. Somehow, in the time it had taken Jim and Jack to update Karen and Jilly, they had returned to the house. Jim could now see the ATV parked in the driveway without the trailer—proof that they were situated somewhere nearby.

Jim and Jack looked at each other with realization in their eyes. Turning back, they saw the three boys walk up the stairs and out of sight. Ten more minutes, and the kitchen and living room lights were turned off. Paul and Tess were getting ready for bed.

Jim felt a poke on his back and turned to see Jack behind him.

"We should get back. It's been a long time, and we need to figure out our next move."

Jim was reluctant to leave without at least knowing where Charlie was, but he knew Jack was right. He was bleary-eyed and frazzled.

They silently backtracked through the woods and found their boat. Untying it, they set off quickly across the lake and then paddled slowly down that side of the lake back to their pier. Tired and achy, they climbed out and trudged back up to the house.

When they entered this time, Jilly was asleep on the couch and Karen was sitting next to her. She looked over her shoulder at them and, again, they shook their heads. Getting up quietly, she walked across the room to greet them.

"Well?" She folded her arms across her chest. Her mouth was set tight, and she looked tired, but alert and angry.

Jack answered.

"Well we found out that he's not being held on their property, which means they're probably keeping it from their parents. Also, they returned to their house in the time it took Jim and me to tell you guys what was happening, get a drink, and get back out there."

"Okay, so where is he?"

Jim had been listening halfheartedly, but something flitted into his mind without conscious thought. He suddenly knew where Charlie was.

"I think I know where. They saw Charlie one day when they were down the lake on the Clarke's land. If they hid him there, nobody would really know. The Clarkes are old and don't get out away from the house much."

Jack looked slightly hopeful. He said, "I haven't been back there in a while. Would they have anywhere to hide him?"

"I have no idea. Wait, yes! I remember hearing that the Clarkes had some things that were vandalized a while back. I think they have a small shed or something back there and maybe some other storage building. I'm just not sure, though."

"That must be it." Jack looked more awake now, but still very tired. His eyes were bloodshot and puffy.

Jim knew he looked the same and felt ten times worse.

"What do we do?" he asked.

Jack took a deep breath and let it out slowly as he thought. "I think that we need some rest. Let's get some rest and then get over there before it's light."

Reluctantly, Jim agreed. They needed to calm down and get some rest. They needed to think.

Jim went upstairs and showered. He felt horrible. He was tired, but he didn't think he would be able to sleep. He had no idea how they were going to make this right. Even if they got him back, how would things be okay with the Whittles? They would make life miserable.

He stumbled over to his bed and fell on top of it. Not even bothering to get beneath the covers, he fell into a light, miserable sleep. He dreamed about Charlie being tortured and then sold. It was horrible.

When he finally awoke with a start, he felt more tired than before. He saw that the sky was beginning to turn. It wouldn't be light for another hour or so, but he could tell it was near. Getting dressed, he could hear little sounds downstairs. Someone else was awake.

When he shuffled into the kitchen, he found his parents there. They had been up all night.

"Hey, didn't you sleep?"

At his voice, they jumped slightly and turned to him.

Jack spoke first. "Hey. No, not really. We both tried." He rubbed his bleary eyes with his hands and then shook his head as if to clear his vision.

"Want something to eat? Drink?" Karen was moving around the kitchen now. She liked to keep busy when she was upset.

"No, thanks. I'm okay." He sat down beside Jack. "Are we going to get Charlie?"

"We're going to try." Jack grimaced and took another sip of coffee.

"What do you think they're doing with him?" Jim was afraid of the answer.

"I think … they're probably going to try to use him to get rich. I think they tranquilized him and are probably keeping him sedated in a shed somewhere."

Karen's voice broke in. "Poor Charlie. He's so sweet and innocent. He doesn't deserve this. He's very important, too, and I don't think the Whittles should have him."

Jim loved hearing Karen voice what he was thinking. His whole family had come to love Charlie in such a short time and this situation was pure agony.

Jack drained his coffee cup and stood up.

"We should go. Karen, be ready in case we need the car. I think we should go from a different direction, and if we get him, we should leave that way too. We'll walk down the road. They're focused on the water and using boats, so they might be thrown off."

Karen moved around to hug each of them.

"Be careful." She gave Jim an extra hug.

"'Bye, Mom."

CHAPTER SEVENTEEN
Re-group

THEY WALKED OUT the front door with Banjo trying to follow them. Jim bent down to see him again.

"Hey, boy. You can't come with us now, but we'll be safe, and we'll bring Charlie back. Don't worry." With a pat, he turned, and they were on their way.

This time, they walked down their driveway and down the road. When they reached the turn, a neighbor's dog walked into their path. It was a yellow lab mix that looked very old. It was never a bother to anyone and just wanted a pet. Jim didn't know her name, so he called her Sunny.

"Hey, Sunny. You be good and stay here, girl." He petted her head and walked on.

Looking back, he saw that she had sat down and was staying. This little act of affection and respect gave him a surge of hope. He felt like even Sunny was on his side, the right side.

They walked quickly and after a while, they came upon the Whittle's driveway. All was quiet there. All was quiet everywhere at this time, but soon many of the neighbors would be up and getting off to work. Being in a rural area, most people worked long distances from home and had long commutes. Paul Whittle was one of them.

Passing the driveway, Jim and Jack moved on. They were now hearing little morning birds chirping as they started the day. As they made their way to the Clarke's, they saw a red fox on the side of the road. It paused for a moment in fear as they walked toward it, then turned and sprinted into the woods. Jim rarely saw red foxes, so he took this to be a sign of good luck.

Finally, they reached their destination. They were going to walk down the Clarke's long, secluded driveway until they reached the house and then turn into the woods for cover. As they walked along, they heard nothing unusual. The woods seemed to be waking up and becoming noisier as the time wore on, which was both good and bad for them.

They reached the small, tidy house and melted into the woods to the left. Neither of them knew where to go or what was out there, but they both headed straight back toward the lake.

After several minutes of walking through some of the thickest brush they had ever encountered, they finally saw the lake. Turning right, they headed parallel to it. The Clarkes owned the land across from the Thomas property, which meant that they owned it all the way down to the end of the Thomas' part of the lake and beyond. Jim and Jack had plenty of land to cover, but they followed close to the lake anyway.

After many more minutes, Jim's eyes were losing focus, and he was losing heart. A chittering sound in the trees above him drew his attention. He paused long enough to watch a couple of squirrels fighting. It was now that time of morning when the light seems blue and the approaching daylight can be felt.

As he turned his eyes back to the front, his mind told him to go back. Looking to the right, Jim thought he saw something unnatural behind a clump of trees. He stopped walking and made a slight clicking sound for Jack to hear.

Jack turned around abruptly and mouthed, "What?"

Jim just pointed. Jack looked for several seconds and then his face brightened with realization. He too saw something that didn't fit.

They veered from their course toward whatever they had seen and soon could make out a green storage shed. It almost looked like a small cabin and may have been used as one in the past, but it was obvious that, in its dilapidated condition, it wasn't used much now. It just *felt* old.

A surge of excitement coursed through Jim as they approached the cabin. Jack motioned to follow him behind a large oak tree.

"We never would have known this was here," Jack whispered into his ear.

"I know, Dad. You think he's in there?"

Jack looked around the tree again. "I see some bikes there. Two."

"What? I didn't see any."

Poking his head around the tree, Jim finally spotted two bikes resting against the cabin. The new mountain bikes were out of place against the old cabin.

"They're already there." Jim couldn't hide his disappointment.

"Just two of them, and this means they still have him here."

"Yeah."

Jim saw that Jack was right, but he wanted them out of there so that there wasn't a fight. He was trying to figure out a way to get them out of there when the door of the cabin opened.

Dave and Sam walked out.

They were talking, but with them facing away, it was difficult for Jim to make out their words. They seemed to be arguing. Dave was doing much of the talking, but Sam wasn't happy. Dave turned to face Sam, so they could now hear his voice.

"I think that university would pay good money for this. I can't believe I almost killed him last night. Luckily, my arrow missed, and now we have this opportunity." He clapped his hands in excitement.

They couldn't quite hear what Sam was saying, but Dave looked disgusted and replied with, "He'll be fine! They wouldn't want to hurt their precious bigfoot specimen. You watch. When Dad finds out, he'll help us find the most money."

Jim and Jack looked at each other. Jack had an "I knew it" look on his face. Jim was really worried about who else already knew about Charlie.

The boys turned and secured the door to the cabin, then got on their bikes and rode off in the direction of the Clarke's driveway.

As soon as Jim and Jack felt it was safe, they went over to the cabin. Looking in the small window, they could see Charlie lying in the back of the cabin. He was still sedated and tied up.

Jim's heart clenched at this sight.

They moved around to the front of the cabin and looked at the lock. It had a padlock on it that required a key to open it. Examining the lock, they saw that the hinge of the hasp was rather old and rusty. If they could break that, they wouldn't even need to unlock the padlock.

Looking around, Jack found a large rock. Walking back to the hinge, he started banging the rock against it. With the first couple of strikes, it looked like nothing would happen, but with the next few strikes, the hinge started coming loose.

"Hey! Get away from there!"

It was Sam and Dave. They were braking to a stop and then threw their bikes down.

"Get away!" Dave was looking snarly.

"Look, boys. He's ours. You kidnapped him, but you can't have him. Leave us alone and there won't be any trouble." Jack had risen to his full height and looked more intimidating than Jim had ever seen him. He practically growled these words. If Jim didn't know him, he would have been terrified of him right now.

There was suddenly the sound of a car engine moving closer. They watched an SUV pull up and Paul Whittle stepped out with John. Paul had a shotgun and marched up to the group. Standing for a moment, he took stock of the situation and then in a horrifying moment, he lowered the shotgun at Jim and Jack.

"Paul, what the hell are you doing?"

"Jack, you need to leave. I know what this is and it's something very valuable. My boys may have been a bit … rash in the way they obtained him, but he's ours now, and you would be best to back off."

"This is wrong, and you know it!" Jack was furious. His face was red, and he looked like he was about to explode at Paul.

"Look, Jack. Just leave before this gets out of hand."

Sam looked horrified. "Dad, let's just be careful here," he said.

"I'm careful, but they need to be careful." Paul was staring stonily at Jim and Jack.

Jack looked around like he was suddenly aware of something.

"This isn't your land or your cabin. I can call about your kidnapping him and stashing him on private property."

"Go ahead! Who would believe you? We have bigfoot for crying out loud! Not to mention I just came from the Clarke's. We had a nice conversation with Mr. Clarke about letting the boys use his land for a, well, we called it a scientific research project. I got written permission." He looked smug.

Jim thought it was amazing how disgusting the prospect of money could make a person.

"Now get off this property." Paul raised the shotgun higher and waited. Their conversation was over.

Jack looked like he was about to say something, but stopped himself. He looked down at his son and said, "Let's go."

Jim was about to protest, but Jack shook his head sharply and nudged him forward. They walked quickly through the woods to the Clarke's driveway. From there, they started a light jog back down the road.

"Dad! They're going to call people and turn Charlie in!"

"I know, I know. I don't think they have yet."

"Why?" Jim was huffing to keep up with Jack's long strides.

"They're just now setting things up with the Clarkes. And Dave was saying something about their dad figuring things out."

"What do we do?"

"Let's think while we go back to the house."

Jim fell silent. His mind was racing. He knew they had to act fast, but didn't know what to do or how to make it all okay again.

CHAPTER EIGHTEEN
Found and then Lost

IT TOOK THEM a while to get back, and by then, Jack seemed to have come up with at least part of a plan. They were going to go back by boat and create a diversion in order to get to Charlie. He would be sedated, so Jack was going to bring their heavy-duty steel yard cart. It supposedly held up to one thousand pounds, so they were hoping that it would carry Charlie easily. To help get Charlie into the cart and the boat, they were taking a page out of the Whittle's book and taking their own ATV loading ramp.

Assuming this went well, they still had to figure out how to keep the Whittles away and out of their lives. One thing at a time, Jim thought.

Reaching their house, they sprinted through the front door. Karen and Jilly were again sitting in the living room, waiting for any word. When they entered, both stood up, but neither asked anything. They could see that things were still very intense and nothing was resolved.

Jilly's face fell. "Oh, Charlie ..." she sighed, slumping back into her chair.

"Jilly, we found where they're keeping him. We're going to get him," Jim promised.

She popped back up from her chair. "I want to help!"

"It's too dangerous," Jack said quickly. "Karen, we need your help."

He explained what they needed from her and then they all moved to get things together for their rescue mission.

As Jim went outside to help get the cart and ramp, Jilly followed. She waited until he was done helping load the ramp into the cart and then tugged on his hand. He bent down to see her.

"Jim, tell Charlie I love him and to come back. And tell the Whittles I hate them." Her little chin trembled, but she was looking strong, resolute.

"I will." He scooped her up in a big hug.

"Let's go." Jack was ready, so they pulled the cart down to the lake. As they walked, Jack said, "I wish I knew what kind of tranquilizer they were using and how to wake Charlie up."

"They're crazy. Who would have animal tranquilizer darts? I knew they were nuts."

"That they are."

They worked in silence as they loaded everything into the boat. A large blanket was put in the bottom of the boat to muffle the sounds, and they quickly got everything into the water. This time they would paddle down the lake. Knowing where the Whittles were, they figured that they were most likely not watching the water, but it was a risk they were just going to have to take anyway.

They paddled quickly and quietly, each going over what they would do in their minds. It was terrifying to know that the Whittles were so unhinged and ready to do harm in order to protect their "valuable" item.

When they reached the spot where they knew the cabin was, they pulled the boat ashore and unloaded the cart. They went as quietly as possible through the woods, making a small loop so that they would approach it from the side and parallel to the lake rather than going straight at it from the lake. This way, they would approach the back of the cabin.

When they felt like they were close enough, Jack sent a text message to Karen. She responded immediately.

They knew that right now, she was making a frantic phone call to the Whittles, telling them that Jim and Jack had gone crazy and were heading to their house right this minute to confront the boys. They had threatened their lives. She had tried to stop them, but couldn't, and she was afraid.

Hopefully this would draw most or all of them to the Whittle house.

Silently making their way closer to the cabin, they now had a good view, so they sat and waited. Within minutes, they heard the door to the cabin crash open. Loud voices rose in the air and then Paul, Sam, and John appeared. They ran to their car, jumped in, and sped off. Dave had walked out to watch them go. Shockingly, they saw he was armed with a pistol.

This was the time. They had to act now.

Jim looked to Jack, who nodded, and they both broke into a quiet run. They flew into the clearing and crossed the distance in seconds. Without speaking, they moved in unison. Dave's attention finally turned away from the car and the commotion at his house, and he seemed to sense or hear them coming. He was too late. They both were on him before he could fully turn around and had him pinned on the ground before he could even make a noise.

He started yelling, but Jim clamped his hand over his mouth quickly. "Shut up!" Dave's eyes were huge, and he stopped squirming for a moment at the ferocious sound of Jim's voice.

Jack was already winding cord around Dave's hands and feet while Jim put tape over his mouth. Dave was immobilized in seconds.

Leaving him on the ground, they ran to the cabin. Entering, they saw Charlie still lying on his side at the back of the cabin. On a small table, there was a vial with a syringe inside it. It looked like they interrupted the Whittles as they were about to give Charlie another dose of sedative. Jim hoped this meant that Charlie would wake soon.

Jim flew to Charlie's side. He put his hands on his big cheeks and called his name. Charlie's eyes were slit open, but he didn't respond. Jack checked that he was breathing and seemed okay otherwise. He nodded to Jim. They cut the ropes binding his legs and arms.

They ran out the door to retrieve their cart and ramp. Time was short, so they were working lightning fast. They ran by Dave, who was trying to worm-wiggle his way to the cabin. Jim kicked him in the rear on the way out and knocked him back on his side.

Bringing the cart around, they pulled it into the cabin. They opened the ramp and began rolling Charlie up into the cart. It was hard work and took a while. He was as heavy as a large football player and didn't fit that well. Jim tried to restrain his legs and arms so that they could move through the door more easily. They had to lean the ramp sort of on top of Charlie, but he seemed okay.

Having secured Charlie, they rolled the cart out the door. Dave was lying there and watching with angry eyes.

"Leave him there," Jack said about Dave. Jim knew he was beyond mad.

They rolled Charlie as fast as they could over the rough terrain. He bumped and bounced along, but still didn't wake. They had to backtrack once when they came up to a clump of branches that were covered in leaves. Finally, they reached the lake. Taking the ramp off Charlie's lap, they unfolded it and positioned it to roll Charlie into the boat. It took some maneuvering, but they got everything lined up and ready to go.

Suddenly, yells broke out behind them. The other Whittles had returned. After a second of fear, Jim and Jack went back to work, focused on the task at hand.

"Hurry!" came a female voice.

They looked up and saw Karen and Jilly standing at the other bank. They were waiting to help with Charlie. Jim saw that Karen had driven their ATV over and had it backed up so that they could use it to haul Charlie back to the house.

Jim and Jack rolled Charlie into the boat without too much trouble. A soft moaning sound escaped from Charlie, who started moving his hands and head a little bit.

He was waking up.

They worked to push the boat all the way into the water, but it was extremely heavy with the cart and Charlie. In fact, it was barely afloat.

Jack pushed the boat into the water the rest of the way and yelled, "Go! I'll swim it!" Hanging on to the boat, he swam along.

Jim paddled harder than he ever had before. Charlie was waking quickly and tried to sit up, but grabbed his head and winced.

Jilly let out a scream, and Karen again yelled at them to hurry.

Listening closely, Jim could hear the Whittles coming closer through the woods. He redoubled his efforts with sweat pouring off his face. His hands felt slick on the oar, but he kept pushing.

"Stop! Stop or we'll shoot!" came a voice behind them.

Jim kept pulling, and they were finally across. Jack pulled himself out of the water, and Karen rushed forward to help. She had placed Jilly behind a tree for cover.

They all gathered around Charlie, who was now able to sit up, and helped him out of the boat. He was leaning heavily on the three of them, but they were able to help him stumble out.

A shot rang out.

They heard the bullet fly through the tree tops overhead. It was a warning shot. "Run!" yelled Jack. He was pulling Charlie along, but Charlie was quickly regaining his footing. They finally got behind the trees and took cover.

Looking out, Jim saw Paul and Dave standing there holding their weapons at the ready. Dave had taken the shot because Paul had his shotgun and the blast would have been different. Oddly, they were looking down the lake and not at Jim and his family.

Jim glanced at where they were looking and saw John and Sam paddling their own boat quickly to meet the others. As they pulled up alongside Paul and Dave, the two of them jumped in. They turned the boat and started to shoot across the lake.

"Let's go!" Jack shouted.

Karen hopped on the ATV and turned the key. They got Charlie and Jilly loaded on and then began to drive away while Jack and Jim began to follow them at a run.

Looking back over his shoulder, Jim saw Dave was standing and leaning frantically to take another shot. Paul saw what he was doing and slapped his arm down.

"Don't shoot them, you idiot!"

Apparently, as much as he wanted Charlie, he wasn't willing to kill people to get him.

The quick, sharp movement sent Dave off balance, and he toppled over the edge of the boat. This sent the boat rocking wildly, and Paul fell against the side of the boat and then over.

The boat was now tipping, and Jim saw Sam throw his arms out wildly, hitting John in the head with the oar. John went limp as the boat turned over, and he disappeared beneath the water. Jim heard another clunk and saw that the edge of the boat hit Sam in the head, and he plunged into the water as well.

"Dad! They're going to drown!"

Jim had stopped. As much as he hated them for what they had done, he couldn't let John and Sam drown. They weren't entirely innocent, but he knew that they really didn't want to do any harm to Jim and his family. Jack stopped, and they saw Dave and Paul crawl ashore on the other side of the lake. They hadn't noticed Sam's and John's peril.

A loud roar erupted from behind them, and Jim turned to see Charlie jump off the back of the ATV. He came bounding back to them with long strides.

"Charlie! Stay back!" Jim yelled, but Charlie ignored him.

He ran past Jim and waded into the water. Jim was scared for Charlie, but right now he was more scared for John and Sam. He didn't want them to die.

Charlie slipped under the water for what seemed like many seconds to Jim. Finally, Charlie came up with Sam. He took a couple of large strokes and pushed him toward Paul and Dave, who waded in to grab him.

Charlie turned and dove underwater again. A few minutes elapsed and Jack dove into the water. He began a smooth swim to where Charlie had disappeared. As he reached the middle of the lake, John popped up from the water. Jack grabbed him and pulled him back to the edge of the lake. Jim helped Jack pull John ashore, but kept looking back for Charlie.

"Charlie! Charlie!" Jilly and Karen were back, and Jilly was rushing toward the water screaming, but Karen pulled her back. "He's drowning! Save him!"

"He's not breathing!" Jack was starting CPR on John, who was pale and limp.

Jim was terrified. John wasn't breathing and Charlie was still under the water. Jack and Karen were helping John, and the Whittles were huddled in pure horror on the other side of the lake. Sam was awake and lying beside them.

Jim dove into the water. He swam out, but Sam yelled at him to stop.

"Jim, no! There are hidden tree limbs under there. I was caught on one, and that thing pulled me out! I would have drowned!"

Jim stopped and tread water. He wanted to save Charlie, but in his heart, he knew he couldn't. It was dangerous, he couldn't see under the dark water, and Charlie was heavy. Charlie could have gotten caught up in the branches, he could have had trouble since he had been sedated just minutes ago, anything.

In a sickening moment of decision, Jim did the hardest thing he ever had to do—he gave up.

Jilly was screaming and crying on the shore. Jim swam back and went to stand with her. He put his arms around her and the tears started flowing freely. He couldn't help it.

They watched as his parents worked on John. Everyone seemed to be holding their breath.

Finally, "He's breathing!" yelled Karen. Jim heard coughing and sputtering. Karen was now cradling his head and rubbing his small cheeks. Jack took her phone and called for an ambulance.

"Jack! Is he okay?" Paul's voice shook, and Jim thought he looked ten years older. He was very white and looked smaller somehow.

"He's breathing. We're taking him down to the end of our driveway to meet the ambulance. Get your family together and get over there."

Paul nodded, and they all disappeared into the woods. Jim knew they were going to get their car and Tess.

Meanwhile, Jim helped his parents put John into the cart and then jumped in beside him. They rigged the cart to be pulled by the ATV, which the rest of the family piled onto.

Driving carefully, they made it back to the house in minutes and went to the end of the driveway to meet the ambulance. Karen sat by John's side, holding his hand. He looked smaller than ever.

Jim stood there, holding Jilly, who was shuddering with each silent sob. He was in shock. Charlie was gone. He had given his life to save the Whittles—the very people who put him through such horror.

They heard a car engine, and the Whittle's SUV appeared from around the corner. The car skidded to a stop in front of the Thomas' mailbox, and the family tumbled out immediately. The Thomas family backed away and let them have their private time with John. A short time later, they could hear the wailing sirens of the ambulance.

CHAPTER NINETEEN
Sadness and Joy

THE PARAMEDICS TENDED to John and swooped him off to the hospital. The Whittles were finally gone, leaving Jim and his family to fully confront the horrors that had transpired. Standing in a daze, they all looked at each other. Without saying a word, they turned and walked slowly back to their house, leaving the ATV and cart behind.

They walked somberly through the front door, where Banjo greeted them with a questioning look. He quickly sensed their mood and plopped down on the floor with a look of sadness.

"Charlie, Charlie, Charlie," Jilly was wailing.

She was crying harder than Jim had ever seen. He looked at his parents and saw them with tears in their eyes too. He couldn't stand this.

Running out the back door, he broke down completely. "Charlie!" He screamed it at the top of his lungs. The tears were hot and seemed to be endless. He collapsed on the deck with wracking sobs.

After what felt like an hour, he was cried out. He sat there, looking out over the backyard with his face pressed against the rails of the deck. He was looking between the slats at the serene view before him. It was amazing how such a horrible thing could happen in a place so full of beauty. The surrounding forest seemed to be unaware of what had happened. Birds were still singing, squirrels were still playing, and he watched a rabbit hop carelessly by.

It was so unfair.

He heard a sound to his left. "Dad, I don't want to talk."

"Jiimmm."

Jim snapped his head around. Charlie was standing there, soaking wet. He had come up the water well trail and stepped onto the side of the deck. Jim's heart flew into his throat, and he felt like he couldn't speak for a second.

"Charlie!" Jim jumped up and ran to him. He jumped into his arms and hugged him as hard as he could. Charlie held him in a tight hug, and Jim felt like his heart would explode.

He heard the back door slide open and then screams of "Charlie!" Suddenly, there were three more sets of arms around both Charlie and Jim. They all stood for minutes, taking in the miracle that was Charlie.

Finally, they pulled away. Charlie looked at the Thomas family with a smile on his face and tears in his eyes. He was rocking from foot to foot and seemed uncomfortable with all the love, but he was also loving it.

"What happened?" Jim shouted. He threw his arms up in a question.

Charlie mimed swimming, and he took a deep breath and held it. He had held his breath and swum away! Jim briefly wondered just how long a bigfoot could hold its breath, but he was too happy to really care.

His family was whole again.

CHAPTER TWENTY
Into the Summer Sun

A WEEK LATER, the Thomas family was in their living room, waiting for an unpleasant meeting. The Whittles were coming over to thank them for what they had done. John was out of the hospital and feeling better. He was going to be just fine thanks to Charlie and Jim's parents.

Jim was sitting in a chair and his legs felt like they wouldn't stop moving. His knee was jumping constantly. He had mixed feelings about seeing these people. Really, he only wanted to see Sam and John, but he had no say in it.

There was a soft knock at the door. Jack crossed the room and opened it.

"Hello! Hello!" Paul said, entering.

There was a jovial chorus of greetings as the Whittle family walked through the door—a little too enthusiastic and happy. Jim assumed it had as much to do with feeling extremely guilty, as it did with John being alive and well.

Paul looked especially guilty. He was forcing the largest smile and looked very anxious and concerned.

They all sat down for some drinks and snacks.

Tess started. "We can't thank you enough for what you did for the boys, especially John. They would be dead if you hadn't been there. I just can't believe they were so careless while they were fishing out there!"

They obviously hadn't told her what they were doing out there or about Charlie. Jack cleared his throat uncomfortably. "We're just glad we could help."

They spoke politely for another fifteen minutes and then the Whittles stood to leave. They wanted to get John home to rest.

Tess went with Karen into the kitchen to get her recipe for the dip she had served. Paul took this opportunity to speak with Jim and Jack about what really happened.

"First, I want to apologize for how we acted throughout the whole ordeal. We were … not thinking clearly and obviously handled everything horrendously."

"To say the least." Jack was not going to make this easy on him.

Jim was angry again. They all thought Charlie was dead, and they weren't even going to mention him?

"Charlie's the one you should thank," he said. "And apologize to."

He looked at each of them. They all shifted uncomfortably and averted their eyes.

John stepped forward. "Jim, I'm really sorry about him. He saved my life down there, and I'll never forget him. Thank you too, Mr. Thomas."

"You're welcome, John. Glad you're okay." Jack looked down at him with a warm smile.

"We're all really sorry, Jim. Even Dave," Sam said. He stepped forward and put a hand briefly on Jim's shoulder.

"Thanks."

Dave mumbled a thanks and continued to inspect the ground.

Paul took a breath and continued. "Look, we're really appreciative of what—it was Charlie you said—what Charlie did for us. For our family. We'll never breathe a word of him to anyone. It doesn't matter anyway, since he, uh, passed away while saving my boys."

Jack finally relented. "We would appreciate that. He was a big part of our lives for a small period of time, but he was amazing and deserves to be left alone, even in death."

"Well said." Paul cleared his throat and looked around again. He blurted out, "We're moving."

Jim was shocked. He blinked in surprise and said, "What?"

"We've been thinking about moving closer to my work anyway, and after all this, well, we need a fresh start. John doesn't want to be here anymore either." John nodded.

Paul lowered his voice and leaned close to Jack.

"Besides, the boys were getting into too much trouble lately. They need to be somewhere we can keep a closer eye on them, ya know?"

Jack just nodded, but Jim couldn't believe it. This, from the man who nearly shot them.

Jack put out his hand. "I'm sure everyone will be sad to see you go. Best of luck and please keep your word, Paul."

Paul took his hand and shook it. "We will. We all would just like to forget about all of this anyway."

"Us too," Jack agreed.

With that, they turned to leave. Tess was happily chatting with Karen as they walked toward the group. She had apparently just broken the news to Karen as well.

"It's going to be a beautiful house. We're going to fix it up a bit, but you should see the kitchen! I'll have to have you over. It'll be so nice being able to run five minutes up to the store instead of having to prepare for the long trek from here." Tess laughed.

"That sounds lovely," Karen said. "You guys will be very happy there." She looked at Jim with a knowing look. He grinned.

They walked them out to their car. As they did, Dave held Jim back.

"Look. I'm really sorry about what I did, and I promise you I'll never breathe a word of Charlie to anyone. He ... he saved my brother's lives. Even after all we did to him." He looked back down again.

Jim gritted his teeth and forced himself to be nice.

"Thanks, Dave. You were excited and got carried away. Good luck."

Dave walked away, and Sam and John moved to Jim. They both thanked him and gave him awkward hugs.

"I'll miss you, man." Sam said.

"You too, Sam, John."

Jim meant it. Despite everything these past few days, he knew they were basically good at heart. Basically.

Finally, the Whittles got in their car and drove away. Jim felt a weight lift off his shoulders and took a deep breath. Looking around, he noticed Jilly was missing. She had slipped away when they were saying goodbye in the house.

He walked to the garage and opened the door.

"Oh, no," he groaned. "Jilly! You can't do that to him!"

She was sitting on a chair and braiding Charlie's hair. He was sitting very nicely and gave Jim an embarrassed shrug.

Jim couldn't help but laugh. He walked in and pulled Charlie's hands to make him stand.

"Come on! Let's go to the fort."

The fort was finally finished and today was the grand opening. Karen had made snacks that she was going to pack into a picnic basket, and they were going to have a celebratory glass of white grape juice. Charlie had loved it when he first tried it the day before. He had nearly purred with content, making Jilly giggle and call him her new kitty.

Charlie turned around and scooped tiny Jilly up into his arms. As he carried her out, Jim grabbed his free hand, and they walked happily out into the summer sun.

www.ingramcontent.com/pod-product-compliance
Lightning Source LLC
Chambersburg PA
CBHW031348170626
46807CB00002B/876